A QUESTION OF

MURDER

ERIC WRIGHT

W☉RLDWIDE®

TORONTO · NEW YORK · LONDON · PARIS
AMSTERDAM · STOCKHOLM · HAMBURG
ATHENS · MILAN · TOKYO · SYDNEY

A QUESTION OF MURDER

A Worldwide Mystery/January 1990

This edition is reprinted by arrangement with Charles Scribner's Sons, a division of Macmillan, Inc.

ISBN 0-373-26039-3

Printed in U.S.A.

---- ★ ----

SALTER PUSHED HIS WAY THROUGH THE CROWD

and left the garage through the Cumberland exit. He walked along the street to the Lilliput bookstore, which was locked up and dark. While he was standing on the steps, peering down, wondering who would want to kill the husband of the bookstore owner with a bomb, unable to believe it was any of the peddlers he had been watching, he became aware of someone behind him, delivering a monologue for his benefit.

"I'm getting out," the voice said. "Could be anybody next. I thought you were looking after us. I'm not stopping here."

It was Vera, delivering herself of her verdict. She was speaking almost quietly, obviously badly frightened. "I knew something was going to happen," she continued. "I knew it. Whoever it is, I'm not going to be the next one he kills."

---- ★ ----

Again, for Valerie

I

ONE

CHARLIE SALTER was feeling his age. On the previous afternoon he had played squash with a trombone player from the Toronto Symphony and been soundly beaten. This he had expected, taking his pleasure from playing over his head with a "B" player who wanted to get in some practice. What had surprised him was that at the end of the game they had been playing for only twenty-five minutes and Salter was as used up as if they had played the full forty. Had he become, at best, a thirty-minute man? Then, climbing the stairs after breakfast, he had failed to lift his foot quite high enough on one step, stumbling significantly; he remembered doing the same thing several times lately on slightly raised paving stones.

He was fit enough—for squash, that is. Activities like gardening, housepainting, and shopping with his wife for wallpaper exhausted him, but he had enough energy for the things he really wanted to do so long as he didn't leave them until too late in the day. Thus, until now, Salter had had an underdeveloped sense of his own mortality, but the squash game and the stumbles made him think.

He tried to consider the problem responsibly. He was now into his fifties. Other policemen his age had already retired, but he was enjoying himself too much to want to do that. Should he, though, before the first heart attack? As usual he found the idea of retirement, like eternity, hard to think about, and he managed it for about five seconds. No, the thing to do was live from day to day. He wasn't due yet. But just having thought about the future even for a

few moments made him feel mature in every sense of th
word.

Annie, his wife, came in from the garden, where she ha
been savoring the beginning of another gorgeous June day
"Your father phoned while you were in the shower," sh
said.

Salter looked at his watch. Nearly time to go to work
"What about?"

"Seth."

"What about Seth?"

"He visited him yesterday. Seth visited your father,
mean."

"Seth? Visited Dad?"

Salter's father lived not far from the streetcar barn
where he used to work, about three-quarters of an hou
away from the Salters' by subway and streetcar. Neithe
Seth, the Salters' fourteen-year-old son, nor Angus, hi
seventeen-year-old brother, had ever shown the slightes
interest in their grandfather, nor he in them.

"He just announced at breakfast that he was going t
visit his grandfather after school."

"Did he know how to get there?"

"I told him."

"What was the reason? Some school project abou
streetcars?"

"Seth's a bit old for projects like that, I think. I don'
know the reason. I didn't want to look too surprised. Kid
are supposed to visit their grandfathers—you know
kindly, twinkly-eyed Grandpa who teaches them how t
make knots and whittle."

"What fairy story is that in?"

The phone rang before Annie could answer. It was hi
father. "One of your boys came to see me yesterday," h
began immediately. "The young one. What's his name?"

"Seth," Salter said.

"That's right," the old man agreed, another irritating habit of his. "What did he come to see me for?"

"I don't know. I guess he just wanted to talk to you."

"What for? Is he all right? P'raps he just wanted to get away from his home for a bit. Is everything all right with you and her?"

"Of course it is. What are you talking about?"

"I was telling May, kids pick up things that you don't realize. I thought p'raps you and her was maybe having a bit of trouble."

"The boy just wanted to visit his granddad. What's so weird about that?" Salter demanded, knowing perfectly well.

"Nothing really, I suppose. He offered to make me a cup of tea, though. Why did he do that? I make the tea here, or May does."

"He was being nice, I guess. He gets it from his mother."

"Did he think we couldn't do it?"

"I don't *know*. Shall I tell him not to come again?"

"Oh, no, no, no. No. As I say, p'raps he just needs to get out of the house, and doesn't have anywhere else to go. No, let him. If he wants to come, that is. Ask him to phone first, though. Especially Sundays. We sometimes have a nap Sunday afternoons. We couldn't figure out who it was banging on the door. I shouted through the door at him at first. I thought it was the Salvation Army, something like that. Told him to come back at the proper time."

"Until you opened the door."

"What?"

"Until you opened the door. Then you saw it was Seth."

"That's right. I could tell by the voice it was just a kid."

"All right. I'll tell him. Everything all right with you?"

"How do you mean?"

"I mean, is everything all right with you?" *You're no* *ill, or cold, or starving, or anything?*

"'Course it is. We're fine. All right, then. Pretty god damn strange, though, isn't it? Just banging on the doo like that? We wondered who it could be."

"'Bye, Dad." Salter put the phone down. Annie wa standing by, waiting for the news. Salter felt the silence o someone listening on the stairs. "That was Dad," he sai loudly. "Saying how surprised and pleased he was at Seth's visit." He shrugged elaborately and pointed to the ceiling Annie, who had heard enough to guess the rest, movec back into the kitchen, grinning.

Salter turned to go up the stairs and was halted by a whisper from his wife. He turned back to see her shaking her head. "Leave him alone," she mouthed.

He joined her by the stove, out of earshot of the second floor.

"What did your father say?"

Salter repeated his father's side of the conversation. "He wants Seth to call ahead before he visits in future," he added.

"I'll tell him. Don't you say anything to Seth."

"Why not?"

"Don't try and explain them to each other. Let them ge on with it."

Salter thought about this for a moment. It was true tha he had been about to try to explain to Seth why and how his grandfather differed from Norman Rockwell's, bu Annie might be right. It was probably time to let him finc out for himself. Feeling mature for the second time tha morning, he kissed his wife on the ear. "This could be in teresting," he said, and left for his office.

THE SPECIAL AFFAIRS CENTER, where Salter worked, was trying to stay clear of the elaborate preparations that were being made for the forthcoming visit of a royal princess. The chief purpose of the visit was to bless the annual running of the Queen's Plate, Canada's most important horse race, scheduled to take place in three weeks' time; but among her other activities the Princess was scheduled to walk around the village of Yorkville, an area of expensive shopping in midtown Toronto.

There had been the usual rumors of attempts to be made on the life of the Princess, but the real task of the police was to organize crowd control for the world's most popular woman. "This'll be worse than the Pope," one experienced officer predicted. "This'll bring 'em *all* out, not just the Catholics." All nonroutine police duties were suspended for the duration of the visit, and every auxiliary officer was asked to turn out. The holdup squad, the bail-and-parole unit, even the harbor police—every special unit on the force contributed manpower to the job of guarding the Princess from her well-wishers. Only the more senior officers had seen anything like it before. "Kosygin was worse," one deputy chief said. "But we could move him about quicker. Had to."

Each day the pool of police concerned with the visit grew larger as the arrangements became more complex and layered. Salter was amazed that the Special Affairs Center was not so far involved. In the original planning, his boss, Superintendent Orliff, had argued that someone had to mind the store, as it were, while the rest of the force worried about the Princess. "Leave us to look after the odd jobs that have to be done," he had said, and he had gotten away with it.

Thus, for several days Salter had been working on a report, a new policy and a set of guidelines for police behavior on picket lines. Many of the police, themselves unionized, disliked monitoring picket lines to control violence and in some jurisdictions in Ontario were virtually refusing to do the job. They disliked it in practice as well as in principle because, however restrained they were, the inevitable scuffles were pounced on by television cameramen who were prepared to wait all day for a shot of police brutality. If a cop separated two men fighting, what appeared on the ten o'clock news was a photo of a policeman with his arm around a picket's neck. And another Post Office strike was looming. Salter had no easy solutions and he was pleased when the phone rang to call him into Orliff's office.

The superintendent looked up from the notes he was making as Salter walked in. "You can leave the picket lines for a while," he said. "A couple of jobs have just come in." He passed over a sheet of paper. "Art fraud," he added. "Someone's been copying our national treasure."

"Why us? Give it to the fraud boys."

"There aren't any at the moment. Everybody's working special detail because of the Princess. Except us. We're still in reserve."

And I'll bet we stay there, Salter thought. He had worked for Orliff for four years now and he understood how the superintendent had managed to stay away from the uproar surrounding the royal visit. Orliff had no enemies, no one who wanted to make his life difficult, no one with a score to settle. He had managed this by having no friends. He was an intensely private man who kept his work and his home totally separate. It had taken Salter two years to learn that the most important of the neat stacks of paper on Orliff's desk consisted of the plans for his retirement cottage. In the office, he worked absolutely by the book, giving Salter his orders with a minimum of explanation, but Salter had known from very early in their relationship that if he did his job well, Orliff would look after him. Orliff nodded now at the paper in Salter's hand. "It's not really our case. We're responding to the Brits, save them sending someone over if they can avoid it. Read it over."

Salter read the document through. It was a summary prepared by Scotland Yard of a possible fraud being perpetrated in Canadian art. For over two years, a trickle of paintings had surfaced in England, oil sketches by well-known Canadian artists of the thirties, painted on cedar shingles, none of them previously catalogued. The provenance of the pictures could not be established (the story was that an old private collection was being sold because the owner was short of money). While the gallery that had sold them could not prove their authenticity, it had put its reputation behind the opinion, confirmed by several experts, that the pictures were genuine, and they had been snapped up at London prices to be sold at better prices in Toronto and Montreal. After two years (and about fifteen pictures had appeared), one that had found a home in a Toronto mansion had been pronounced fake. The painting, it was demonstrated, could not have been painted by that particular artist because an important detail of the scene had not existed when he was alive—this according to one of the artist's descendants, a lady who was writing his biography. The investigation had cast doubts on all the newly discovered paintings, and the gallery was very worried. The English police traced them to a dealer in Upper Slaughter who insisted that he received them, complete with attribution (but without signatures) from an agent in Switzerland.

Attached to the document was a photograph of the painting showing a typical scene in Ontario's lakeland—

water, trees, a rocky shoreline, and a sky, all disturbed by an autumn wind, a picture of a kind familiar to every Canadian child from the walls of his schoolroom. The unusual feature of this scene was a small wooden church, perched on an island.

"It's a place called Stoney Lake," Orliff said. "That church is called St. Peter's-on-the-Rock. Now, see that cupola or coopola or whatever the hell it's called, that belfry thing? It was only put on after the war, when this artist was dead. The roof fell in apparently and when they got around to rebuilding it they stuck that thing on top. Those little black stripes are the giveaway."

"I'll talk to her. Where does she live?"

"Rosedale. It's on the sheet," Orliff smiled. "Then maybe go up there, find someone painting pictures of the shoreline. Tell him we're on to him."

"And bring him back?"

Orliff shook his head. "No. Even if you actually find the guy, he may be doing nothing illegal. Unethical, yes. But find out where the pictures go from him. Somewhere along the line someone is working a swindle. It's the guy who actually says that the pictures are authentic that the Brits want. Anyway, go through the motions. Could be a nice little day out at the lake. Now, here's the other one."

Salter laid the art fraud aside and took the second paper from Orliff. Attached to it were five sheets of notepaper.

"Threatening letters," Orliff said, "The story's on television already."

Salter read the summary. Five merchants in the Yorkville area had received letters threatening to disrupt their businesses unless street traders were allowed to operate freely in the village. The letters were identical, all signed

"The Street Traders of Yorkville." Salter sniffed them. "Perfume," he said.

"Finish reading."

The report described an ongoing tension between the merchants and the street vendors that had persisted over several years, as the merchants tried to persuade the city to ban the street traders entirely, and succeeded in cutting down their numbers. The threats presumably came from among those traders who had been denied permission to sell in the area. The account ended with a memo from the provincial laboratory that the notepaper was a common one, there were no fingerprints, and the perfume was called Joy.

"A woman?"

"I wouldn't count on it these days."

"I used to live in Yorkville twenty-five years ago," Salter said. "With my first wife."

Orliff looked politely interested, but said nothing.

Salter looked out at the blue sky and grabbed an opportunity to go for a walk in his old neighborhood. "I'll get over there right away."

"No rush. Whoever wrote them is probably satisfied now. Like the guys who get their jollies making obscene phone calls. But yeah, sure, show the shopkeepers we care. Give me a report this afternoon. What's Gatenby up to? You could send him."

Sergeant Gatenby was Salter's assistant. "He's on leave," Salter said. "Right now he's in Oregon on his way down the west coast in a Volkswagen camper."

"I thought all leave was canceled until the visit's over."

"He got away just in time."

Orliff laughed. "Cute bugger. We should have gone with him. So let me know if you find out anything. Yorkville is

where Her Highness is going to walk about, so we have to
be a bit careful.'' He nodded Salter away.

Salter returned to his office for his jacket, locked the
report on picket violence in a drawer, and set off for
Yorkville.

TWO

HE STROLLED along Bloor Street, past the Bay store, looking at the street traders with a fresh eye. There were several outside the Bay and a sprinkling lining the curb all the way to Bellair. Handmade jewelry predominated, but the traders were selling a lot of other things—T-shirts, postcards, belts, scarves. None of the peddlers looked sinister. What struck him was how many of the women ignored the public in order to read—mostly small, closely printed books. Those who weren't reading were standing by their wares like most of the men, staring into space like nineteenth-century day laborers waiting to be hired. They certainly weren't bothering the pedestrians as far as he could tell, but then, the pedestrians weren't complaining, either. He walked down Bellair to Cumberland Avenue, past a row of traders lining the parking lot, until he was almost at Avenue Road, standing across from a huge condominium which had replaced his old apartment block.

Any historian wishing to chart the social trends of the last thirty years would find Yorkville an ideal focus for his studies. Salter had watched the "village" go through two major shifts of identity since he first lived there. In 1960 it was possible to rent a place to live in Yorkville as cheaply as anywhere else in midtown; there were still pensioners on Yorkville Avenue and the streets north of it who had lived in the same rented cottages all their lives. The quarter was popular then with the students from the University of Toronto. It was handy for the university, the "King Cole" beverage room, and Palmer's, the best lunch counter in

Toronto. The Salters had once had friends on Hazelton Avenue, living in a slightly ramshackle block now the site of Hazelton Lanes, perhaps the most upscale shopping mall in Canada. Then the first coffeehouse, the Penny Farthing, opened up across the street from the Salters' apartment, and the flower children arrived. The alternative culture took over the area, and for a year or two the village was synonymous with incense, folk songs, and marijuana. Then on summer nights Yorkville was the closest thing to a piazza Toronto has ever had as people from the suburbs came to town to watch the hippies at play. A number of merchants opened up more conventional stores to tap the tourist traffic and the second revolution began. Property prices rose, slowly at first, then with gathering speed as the bead and macramé shops left to be replaced by couturiers and clothing designers. The yuppies filled the gap left by the hippies, and courtyard cafés featuring reggae music replaced the old coffeehouses. The area is now held in contempt by the artistic community, who have moved to Queen Street in search of the real Toronto, but traces of the previous ages can still be found, in the basement stores and along the rooftops where one or two of the old cottage chimneys survive. And middle-aged relics of the sixties can still hope to find someone they know drinking coffee in the area, except on Sundays when the village, like the rest of Toronto, is closed.

Salter had enjoyed living here until his first marriage broke up, and he still liked visiting it. It felt to him like the center of town.

At nine-thirty the area was quiet—few of the merchants opened until ten—but a row of traders had already set up on the south side of Cumberland. The pedestrians around were mostly tourists from Buffalo and Detroit, waiting for the Canadian shopkeepers to wake up and sell them something. Salter watched a yellow patrol car cruise slowly along the street, beginning the day's ticketing of parked cars. The cruiser pulled level with the row of peddlers and the driver looked along the row, apparently counting heads, while the traders ignored him. When he was satisfied, the policeman turned left onto Bellair to begin a circuit of the block which would bring him back every fifteen minutes to the traders. None of the stores Salter had to visit looked open, so he bought a morning paper, threw away most of it, and took the remainder to an outside table of a café. Five minutes later he was having such a nice time, drinking coffee and reading an article about how much his house had increased in value in two years, that he nearly forgot what he was there for. The stream of store owners passing with their take-out coffee brought him back to his work, and he consulted his list.

The first store was nearby, a boutique called Vera's, with a gray-and-white picture-frame window through which could be seen a single silk dress hanging in an antique pine wardrobe. Before calling on the proprietor, Salter took one more look at the quiet row of traders, now beginning to attract a little business. At this hour they were giving the tourists something to do until the regular merchants opened up. So far, Salter was unable to see what the merchants were concerned about.

Vera was a tall, dowdy woman with graying black hair cut in a fringe above her eyes, and flat on top as if she carried baskets of dresses on her head. She seemed to Salter an odd-looking person to be running a high-fashion boutique, and he wondered if the idea was that she would make her customers feel soignée by comparison. Salter introduced himself and asked her if she had any idea who sent the letter.

"Of course I do. That shower out there," she said, gesturing at the traders. Her voice was noisy and her accent English of a superior kind but not, to his ear, upper class. She sounded to him like a transatlantic telephone operator.

"What's the problem?" Salter asked, perhaps unwisely.

"The problem? I should have thought that was obvious. Those buggers are threatening me. They need to be cleaned out right now."

"No, I mean the problem in the first place. How are they interfering with you? I presume they know you've complained?"

"In the first place they are competing with me. They don't have the overheads, rent, anything like my expenses. That's one problem."

"None of them are selling dresses," Salter said gently.

"I sell scarves and sweaters, too. But all right, they are really competing with some of the other people more. My problem is that they clutter up the place. My customers should not have to wade knee-deep through half-eaten hot dogs on a street full of beggars. That's not what this store is about."

Salter walked to the door and looked out. "Where are the hot dogs?" he asked.

"Come back on Monday morning after the weekend," she said. "I have to sweep them off the steps and wash the sidewalk before I can open up. They use those steps like a park bench. And they set up their bloody stands in the sidewalk, right outside the door, so that you can hardly get into my shop. Then they want to use my washroom."

"That's all stopped now, though, isn't it? I mean you've won. No one is allowed now except those people over there."

Vera flung her arm in the direction of the traders across the street. "I want those moved out of here, too. They don't belong in an area like this. But I've been through all this, over and over. Now these letters. Surely you're going to do something?"

"We have to find out where they came from first."

She closed her eyes in a God-give-me-patience gesture.

"Where the hell do you think they came from? Those people are bloody terrorists. Are you going to wait until they start throwing rocks? I thought this was a civilized country. People here are always bragging about it. So safe, they say. Bloody well looks like it, doesn't it? And where are these people getting their stuff? Half of it is stolen. Off the back of a lorry, you can be sure." On she went, and Salter, who had recognized an obvious target for a civic-minded assassin in the first minute, listened with half an ear and got out as soon as he could.

Three of the remaining four—a luggage shop, a costume jeweler, and a restaurant—were as hostile as Vera without her talent for vituperation, while the last one, an Italian men's clothing store where Salter saw a shirt on sale, half-price, for seventy-five dollars, was a puzzling choice of targets because the owner was only barely aware of the street traders. He had first noticed them when he got a threatening letter, and up to that point he had not cared in the least if there were peddlers in Yorkville.

"You don't think they would bother your customers?" Salter asked.

"I don't have customers. I have clients and they don't care what is in the street."

Unsure what this meant, Salter accepted the man's word that he didn't care, either. His first check over, he spent an hour wandering the area, shuffling like a tourist from peddler to peddler, then turned into an antique store on

Yorkville. The owner, Jenny Schurman, was an old friend of his wife's, and had several times helped Salter to pick out gifts for Annie, even keeping back items from the stock that she knew Annie might like, ready for the next anniversary. She saw Salter coming and called to him from the back of the store.

"Had lunch?" Salter asked, accepting a kiss on the cheek.

"I can't get out. Why don't you get us a sandwich from the Coffee Mill? I'll make some tea."

Salter went off and returned with two meat-loaf sandwiches on rye, and a small cream cake for her dessert. Jenny looked at the cake and put it in a drawer. "I'll give it to the janitor's little girl," she said. "What are you doing around here? Where's Annie?"

"I'm on duty. Looking for a madman among the street traders. You wouldn't happen to know who is behind these notes? Save me a lot of trouble."

"Are you worried? They seem to me like someone working off a bit of frustration."

"Anything that comes within a hundred miles of being a threat to Her Highness we have to worry about." Salter looked out at the tourists window-shopping their way along the street. "You remember when this place was nothing but peddlers?"

"Oh, sure. All selling each other tie-dyed T-shirts. That's when I bought this building."

"What did it cost you?"

"Fifty thousand. My father said I was insane."

"What's it worth now?"

"One and a half million."

"It's long way from the kids with guitars, isn't it?"

"That's all gone. You have to sell a hell of a lot of crafts to generate a rent of fifty dollars a square foot. I should move, take my profits, but I can't see myself on Queen Street.''

"How do you feel about these peddlers? Do they bother you?''

She shrugged. "I'm ambivalent. Maybe they're part of the color, though I don't think they attract many of my customers. I'm glad I'm not competing with them, but, as my sister reminded me last week, that's how our grandfather started when he came over from Poland. He used to sell needles and thread from a handcart. He ended up owning three office blocks downtown. So I don't like to get snotty about them, and I haven't signed any petitions. I wouldn't want the place overrun with them, though. Now I have to go. I've got customers.'' She got up, kissed him, wiped a crumb off his face, and disappeared into the shop.

Salter left the store and bought a paper cup of coffee on his way through the arcade to Cumberland, where he found an empty bench by the parking lot. He drank his coffee and watched the traders selling their wares. It was time to do some homework.

The normal place to start was the local police division that looked after the district, but Salter thought he had a better idea. He phoned City Hall and asked to be connected to his first wife, who worked for the mayor as a community organizer, and with whom Salter had recently gotten on good terms again. Who at City Hall, he wanted to know, could tell him the most about the dispute?

"Fitch,'' she said. "Ed Fitch. He's not the councillor for Yorkville but he headed up the committee which sorted out the problem last summer. He's got the whole thing in his head. He's just in his first term so they stick him with everything. He's okay. A bit gung-ho, but in the right way. Want me to set up an appointment? I can walk down the corridor to him.''

"I'd like to see him this afternoon."

"Call me back in ten minutes."

Salter did as he was told and was booked to see the councillor in an hour.

"Thanks," he said. "How's it going, Gerry?"

"I thought you'd never ask. Fine. I'm still here. I'm not getting married again. No serious diseases. You know. Fine. And you?"

"All of those, and still married."

"How is . . . Annie?" she asked.

"She's fine. How's your boy?"

"He's fine. Everything's fine, I guess."

"See you, then," he said, after a few moments.

"Right. See you, Charlie."

He hung up. He was glad she was fine. He had no desire to see her again, or, he assumed, she, him. As long as they were both fine.

ED FITCH was a small, cheerful man known to Salter only slightly by reputation. He was very popular, a man of the people who magnetized those he touched in such a way that he was already gathering a permanent force of loyal workers around him large enough to support a run for mayor when he had served his apprenticeship. Salter had heard people speak of Fitch in a worshiping way that put his teeth on edge, but meeting him now he found himself drawn to the man. Before they got down to business, Fitch asked him where he was from, where in Toronto he was born, that is, just as if the two Torontonians had bumped into each other in Central Africa. Fitch then spent some time trying to decide if they had ever played on the same Little League team in their different eras. It all took no more than five minutes, and there was nothing phony about it, and Salter saw how hard it would be not to vote for the man once you had had your five minutes.

"The street traders," Fitch said, getting down to business. "Let me ask you something first, Charles. Do you think they are being victimized? Poor little guys trying to make enough for a night's lodging being pushed away by the big, fat, greedy rich bastards of Yorkville?"

"I did this morning but I've had a good look at them and they don't look too deprived."

"Good for you, Charles, good for you. I was riding around on a white horse myself until I found out that one of the traders is putting himself through medical school selling sweaters—listen to this—sweaters he buys from his father cheaper than his old man sells them to his Yorkville customers so the kid can *sell* them cheaper than *they* can *buy* them. The kid drives an Audi." Fitch bounced around in his chair in glee. "I got very objective after that," he added, still grinning. "So what can I do for you?"

Salter showed him the five letters. Fitch's eyebrows shot up. "They're playing rough now, are they? So how can I help?"

"Fill me in. What's the war about?"

Fitch trotted around his desk. "The problem starts here," he said, leading Salter to a large framed map of the city, hanging on the back wall of the office. "See, the city administers Yorkville, but the main streets like Bloor and Bay are Metro roads."

Salter nodded, aware of the quaint device by which the City of Toronto and Metropolitan Toronto, a super-council set up by the provincial government, were two separate jurisdictions.

"So we can control the traders in the village, as we have," Fitch continued, "but not the ones on Bloor Street. That's Metro. We've issued vending licenses to eight traders on Cumberland and a few other odd spots. And that's it. It's a saw-off. The regular merchants don't want any traders at all, but there are two hundred peddlers who'd like to get into the area. They're part of the crowd on Bloor Street where you've got traders with licenses but with no assigned spots. These people can be fined for obstructing traffic, and when the merchants put too much pressure on you guys, that's what happens.''

''Who's sending the threatening letters?''

''Not the traders in the village. They're okay. Any of the others, I guess. You think it's serious?''

Salter considered this. ''No,'' he said. ''No, I don't. But it doesn't make any difference what I think. With Her Royal Highness coming we have to act as if it is.''

Fitch made a face. ''Maybe we should've let the Harbourfront people have her.'' Harbourfront was the name of a collection of renovated warehouses along Toronto's reclaimed waterfront which had been made over into a shopping district. ''The Harbourfront Association made a bid to have her visit the waterfront. There was a real battle. Even the Italians along St. Clair put in a bid. I was chairman of the committee set up to arbitrate that one, too. We eliminated the Italians—they got the Queen the last time around—but it was close between the other two. I cast the deciding vote. I'll remind them the next time I want something.'' Fitch grinned again.

Fair enough, thought Salter. Apart from being called Charles, he was liking Fitch. ''You see the problem,'' he said. ''These people could get the idea that a good day to raise a fuss would be when the Princess was walking round the village. They might not have thought of it yet, or they wouldn't have sent these letters.''

Fitch nodded. ''But you have, and *they* will eventually.''

"Did you meet many of these traders? The ones who applied for licenses? Did any of them seem to you like the ones I should start with?"

Fitch shook his head. "We laid down the principles and City Hall gave out the licenses in the regular way. I met a few of the deputations. They seemed like just plain folks with a complaint, is all. I was more intimidated by a couple of the merchants."

They were interrupted by a secretary, and Fitch looked inquiringly at Salter to know if they were finished. Salter got up to go. "This Yorkville Festival," he asked, buttoning his coat. "This an annual thing?"

Fitch grinned. "It is now. The merchants invented it when they heard the Princess was coming. The way they are talking now, you'd think it went back to Confederation." He glanced at the waiting secretary and back to Salter.

"Thanks for the time," Salter said.

"My pleasure, Charles." Fitch shook hands across the desk. "Anyway I had to see you. Gerry ordered me to, and if I don't keep in with her, I'm dead." It was a joke that contained an invitation to chat about Gerry, but Salter closed it down. "I didn't know she was that important," he said.

On his way out of the building he called on the department responsible for processing the applications for peddlers' licenses and asked permission to borrow the file containing the rejected applications. Back at headquarters he set a clerk to photocopying the contents of the file.

"What are you going to do with that?" Orliff demanded to know. "You going to try and question them all? It'll take weeks."

"The threatening letters are typed. I want to send them, along with this bunch of applications, over to the lab to see if they can match anything up. The crime lab is still working, is it? They aren't in uniform, getting ready to guard the Princess, are they?"

Orliff laughed. "They are going to love you for this," he said.

For the next two days, Salter walked around Yorkville, talking to the patrolmen who had the job of issuing tickets to the peddlers on Bloor Street. None of them could offer a particular trader or group of traders as being more aggressive, thus more suspicious, than the others. And the response from the lab was negative.

"Anonymous letters are always impossible to trace unless you have a suspect," Orliff said. "I'll send a report up to the War Room, then file it until we get something to go on. What about the art fraud case?"

"I'll go and see her tomorrow."

"Keep busy, or you'll be sucked into the rest of the fun and games upstairs."

THREE

AT TEN O'CLOCK the next morning Salter was interviewing, or being interviewed by, Mrs. Beldin, a gray-haired lady in a blue linen dress whose great-uncle had not painted the picture attributed to him. The large stone house stood on adequate grounds on a choice site overlooking a ravine. A million? Salter wondered. A million and a half? The lawn in front of the house was neatly kept, and some flowering shrubs edged the sidewalk, but there were no other flower beds, nothing requiring daily care. Instead, the grounds, front and back, were decorated with a dozen stone ornaments—a sundial, several nymphs, a gargoyle, and a number of mythical animals including a sphinx and a griffin. There was no lawn furniture or any other evidence that anyone used the garden. Inside, the house was as cold as a cellar and seemed untouched by fashion, as if it had been opened recently after a long sleep. The living room was furnished with wing chairs upholstered in faded blue plush, flanked by glass-topped side tables. The pinkish broadloom was slightly discolored in places but still thick and good for another fifty years.

"What do you know about Canadian art, Inspector?" she asked as soon as they were seated. "The Group of Seven?"

"I know Tom Thomson was drowned in Canoe Lake."

"He wasn't one of the Group. Do you know Stoney Lake?"

"No."

"Right. Here are some photographs of my great-uncle's paintings. Now here's the picture you've already seen. See the difference?"

"No."

"Of course you don't. There isn't any. This forger is good. Now Stoney Lake. Let me tell you about it." She uncrossed her legs and leaned forward with her elbows resting on her knees, her hands clasped together. "My family has been connected with Stoney Lake since the twenties. In those days people used to go up by train to Lakefield and take the steamer to their island. Later on we went by car along Highway Two and stopped at Welcome for lunch. Used to take us about six hours. My great-grandfather bought an island there and built a summer home. As each of his children married, he built them a cabin on the island so that he could have his family around him during the summer."

"How many?"

"There are five cabins now. I still use the main cottage but I've had to board up the others. My great-grandfather had two sons and four daughters, the sons being my grandfather and his brother, Amis, the painter. Amis quarreled with his father and was thrown out of the family. They were never reconciled, so he never came up to Stoney Lake again."

"What was it about? The quarrel."

"We never found out. My great-grandfather refused to talk about his son, and my grandfather—rather a weak man, I think—kept away from knowing anything about his brother. When Amis died, in poverty, they found a novel in manuscript among his things which might have told us but his sisters found it too autobiographical and burned it, and that was that. The point is that Amis never returned to Stoney Lake and he died long before the roof was re-built.''

What Salter was hearing was much more absorbing than what he was supposed to be listening to. He accepted Mrs. Beldin's proof of the forgery immediately; what interested him was the glimpse he was getting into the social history of her family. Thus his next question had nothing to do with the painting. ''You live here?'' he asked. The place seemed to him like a museum. ''In the winter, I mean? I was given two addresses for you.''

''I don't live here at all, except for a week or so a year to check that it's all right. It is my house: I pay the bills. But my daughter lives here. When my husband died, I moved out.''

Salter waited for more.

''I was tired of keeping house, you see. My daughter was obviously never going to marry and I could foresee a dreary future of cooking her dinner every night when she came home from the library where she works. I couldn't ask her to leave, could I? She was born in this house. I live in a service flat now where I can eat in the restaurant or have things sent in.''

''So it's your daughter's house?''

''No, it's my house. If she decides to leave I'll move back in. But I'm not going to spend the rest of my life accommodating to someone else. I had enough of that. I pay the bills and the gardener and the cleaning woman and so on. But I can't offer you a cup of coffee because my daughter has put locks on all the cupboards. She suspects the cleaning woman of stealing things. Tea bags. She's on a very small budget, you see.'' The woman looked at him inquiringly, waiting for his next question, folding her hands in her lap.

Salter gazed out of the window to make sure he was still living in Toronto. "Sensible girl. Now, how do I get up to Stoney Lake?"

She opened a bureau and gave him a copy of an old, handmade map. "You can use the 401 now. It wasn't built when we made these maps for our friends, but once you get to Peterborough you'll find the map still works."

Salter stood up.

"Another thing that forger got wrong," she added. "The title."

Salter looked at the picture. "What's it say? I can't read it."

"St. Peter's on-the-Rock, Stony Lake," she read out. "No 'e' in Stony. No one in our family would spell it that way."

"That's how it is on the map," Salter pointed out.

"The map is wrong. It was made by a neighbor at the lake who didn't know any better. But everyone in my family knew how to spell it." She folded the map and put it in his hand. "Let me know if you catch him. It'll make a nice little footnote in my next chapter." As she let Salter out the door she added, "By the way, the lake has magic properties. Perhaps if you sit still in your boat—you'll need a boat to see the church—you'll get a vision of the forger. Good luck."

From Rosedale, Salter drove down to Dundas Street to visit the art gallery where he spent a couple of hours looking at Canadian art and reading what he could find about the artist, Amis Settle. After that he was ready as he would ever be to do the rounds of the dealers. First, though, he decided, he would take up Orliff's suggestion. First he would get in a day's fishing on Stoney Lake.

"Do you think Grandfather would rather have a kitten or a puppy?" Seth asked the table at dinner that night. There was a silence while each member of the family searched faces to see if anyone else knew what Seth was talking about. Salter said, "How do you mean? Who says he wants either? We never had cats or dogs around when I was a kid."

"I read an article in the paper this morning. This doctor said that old people get lonely but it helps if they have a pet. I thought I would get him one from the pound."

"That's nice, but first of all, I don't think you should talk about him as 'old people.' Not to his face, anyway."

"Why?"

"Because you'll offend him. He isn't used to the idea of being old. He may never get used to it. And second, he isn't lonely. He's got May." May was his father's girlfriend, the widow of a former fellow worker, with whom he lived.

"But she never says anything."

"Not when we're around, but she probably talks a blue streak when they are alone."

"Is grandfather sexually active?"

Annie moved quickly to clear the dishes, helped by Angus's girlfriend. Salter was alone with his sons. "Was that in the article, too?" he asked.

"Yes. It said that many people were sexually active into their seventies. Is he?"

Angus laid his head sideways on the table, his face red, and waited, with Seth, for a reply.

"You mean could he be? According to your doctor, apparently yes. That's medical. I don't know if he *is*, though. That's personal, something we don't chat about." There. A little lesson. Salter felt proud of himself. It was not true, though, because ever since he had taken up with May, his father had made it clear to Salter that he had become invigorated, thus in his old age parading the subject that had never been allowed out of the bedroom in Salter's youth.

Salter searched for an exit from the topic. "What's it all about, anyway? Why this concern for your grandfather?"

"Why not? I don't think we care enough for our old people. I feel sorry for grandfather."

"Do you," Salter said, seeing the statement as a personal attack on him. Since Salter's marriage, his father had never been an easy guest in his son's house. Annie worked hard to do her duty by the old man, but he refused to relax with her, forever on the alert for signs that he was being patronized. Salter could think of nothing that would enrage the old man more than the knowledge that Seth was feeling sorry for him. "Don't let him know it," he said.

Annie returned from the kitchen and distributed ice cream all around. When they were all seated again, she asked, "How are things at work, Charlie? Are we going to get away to the Island on time?"

"If not, you can go ahead. I'll follow as soon as I can."

"We should take Grandfather and May," Seth said. "We always leave them behind."

Now Salter had him. "We asked him. He said no. We always ask him. He always says no. If we didn't ask him, though, he'd get upset. This way everybody's happy."

"Why? Don't you want him to come?"

"Look, kid. Give up, will you? Wait until you have to cope with me and you'll understand."

Seth looked at Angus for support to continue the argument, but he was some months too late, for Angus had grown up and changed sides. Eventually, he said, "I'm still going to see him. He's my grandfather," and left the room.

Annie said, "It's a stage he's going through. At his age I wanted to be a nun."

"What happened?"

"I got as far as being confirmed, then I learned to ride, so I decided to be a vet instead."

"What case are you working on now, Mr. Salter?" Angie smiled at him, interested, courteous, deferential.

Angus's girlfriend was a pretty, tanned blonde, dressed like Angus in baggy khaki clothing so that the two of them sometimes looked interchangeable. Her name was Angela, shortened to Angie, further emphasizing their Pierrot/Pierrette image. Apart from some very minor skirmishes with girls, incidents which Salter suspected were no more than sexual test flights, Angus had not had a real girlfriend until now, but the involvement with Angie was entire and complete. After school they moved as a single unit: Like a pair of khaki-colored fish, they swam through and around Salter's world, self-absorbed and self-sufficient. Their relationship did not seem to depend on touching. They were able to meet and part without a kiss or a sigh, seeming permanently and profoundly connected by some kind of force, like twins. When he got home from school, she was sitting on the front garden wall, waiting. If she was not there, he got on his bike and went to find her. They had known each other for three months, and it looked as though only a war or a plague would part them. Watching them and remembering how awkward he had been with his own first girl, Salter was envious, though happy for Angus. The lives of the two adolescents seemed to have intersected at exactly the right point to allow them to be siblings, children, lovers, friends, all at once; they had met on the day before the Fall and stayed there in an eternal Now. So far, anyway. "There was a couple like that at university," Annie once said. "They came together like magnets in first year and stayed that way until they graduated, forsaking all others."

Salter told them about the threatening letters.

There was a long pause. Then Angie asked, "Do you believe in capital punishment, Mr. Salter? I know most policemen do."

"Most police *spokesmen* do. They are the ones that get reported. The rest of us blow about as hot and cold as the public."

"What about you?"

"I'm not going to tell you, because you don't know me well enough. What about you?"

"My father says they should execute all child murderers."

"That's because your father has children. What about you?"

"I don't know. Even child killers must be sort of sick, don't you think?"

"Probably. There's only one category that most cops think should be executed."

"Who are they? The ones who kill policemen?"

"No. Professionals. People who kill for money. Most of us think that if they knew they were going to die they wouldn't be so keen to take up the trade. See, if you offer someone fifty thousand dollars to kill someone else, he figures that's pretty good odds. Even if he's caught, he's got a nice little nest egg for when he gets out. Most of us hate professionals worse than cop-killers."

"Hmmm," Angie said, politely.

That was enough of Salter's world for one summer evening. Angus, who had moved around behind Angie while she was listening, said, "By the way. We're not coming to the Island this year."

"Who's 'we'?"

"Angie and me. We're staying home. We'll look after Clem and the house. We've got jobs at Ontario Place for the summer."

"Doing what?"

"Angie is on the garbage squad, and I'm selling hot dogs."

There was a lot for Salter to sort out about this news. He reacted first to the "we" of Angus's opening sentence, wanting to point out that Angie, nice as she was, had not, in fact, been invited to join them on the Island. Second, neither the house nor Clem the cat needed looking after— the neighbors always took care of both. Third (and here was the one that was first on Salter's list), what did Angus have in mind while they were away? Twenty-eight days roistering in Salter's bed? What the hell was going on? But he knew enough to begin his inquiries later, with Annie. For the moment he just said, "Is that right? Well, well," and glanced sideways at Angela, who was eating ice cream with aplomb. Salter was confused.

When he and Annie were alone, he asked, "Are we going along with this?"

"What?"

"Those two, here, on their own, while we're away?"

"Should I get a baby-sitter?"

"All right, all right. But is it okay? I mean, *Jesus*?"

"I'll think about it. Angus is seventeen."

"That's what I mean. He's seventeen! Just, for God's sake. How old is she?"

"Seventeen. Just, I suspect. Look, I don't know what you want me to say. I'll think about it. It's news to me, too, you know. But I don't know what we can do about it, if anything, or if we should."

FOUR

SALTER ARRIVED at the office the next morning to find a message that Orliff wanted to see him as soon as he came in. When Salter walked in, Orliff handed him a bundle of papers without speaking.

Salter picked them up. "New letters?" He read the top one through. It was identical in wording to the previous letters. The paper was different, and there was no perfume, but otherwise the two groups were the same.

"When did they come?"

"Yesterday. I sent a lad over to pick them up. You'd better get after it right away. She's coming in two weeks. I've got two men looking after the peddlers."

Salter did not need to be told. A second group of letters had to be taken seriously, something more than a gesture of frustration or misery. He put the letters in his pocket and made to leave.

"I want to know by tonight what we should do about them," Orliff warned. "I haven't told the War Room yet. I will on Monday. All right?"

"I'll report back this afternoon."

When he compared the two groups of letters back in his office, one other discrepancy emerged. Four of the recipients were the same, but one, the Italian tailor, had been dropped and another added. The new one was Lilliput, a children's bookstore on Cumberland. Salter decided to tackle it first.

THE STORE was in a basement, and when Salter walked down the steps a slightly plump woman in her early forties with brown hair pulled back into a smooth bun was struggling to turn the lock while balancing a cup of coffee. Salter took the coffee away from her and the lock immediately yielded to the right pressure. She let him in, resecured the lock, turned on the lights, and dropped her keys on the desk. Salter was waiting when she looked up.

"Can I help you?" she asked him. Round-faced, with a high color and some suntan, she had a glowing, expectant look. Her diction was precise; her manner, eager to be of service.

Salter explained himself and her eyebrows shot up. "I'm all alone at the moment."

The first customers, an American family, were already coming down the steps.

"Can you come back when it might be a bit quieter? This looks like being a busy morning. Oh, hang on a sec. Here's Tommy."

A cheerful-looking man, about the same age as the woman, bounced in. Nearly bald, with steel-rimmed glasses and dressed in a yellow cotton sweater, gray trousers, and red-and-white running shoes. "Ruthie," he cried. "I bring you muffins and coffee. Oh, you already *have* coffee. No fair. You've spoiled my lovely gesture. Never mind. I'll drink it myself. Like my sweater? And my shoes? I'm sick of being gloomy. I want to sizzle." He turned to Salter. "Hi," he said, smiling full-face at the inspector from three feet away, like a favored child entering its parents' bedroom.

"Hi," Salter replied, stepping back a pace.

The bookstore owner introduced everybody. "Tommy Nystrom, Inspector Salter, and I'm Ruth Pearson."

The man raised his hand level with the top of his chest and pushed it forward, smiling. "Hi," he said again.

"Hi," Salter said and shook his hand.

"Look after the cash for a moment, Tommy," Ruth Pearson said. "I'll talk to the inspector in the back."

Salter followed her into a tiny office/storeroom lined with shelves of stock, and with a large desk filling half the room. Ruth Pearson perched herself on a stool; Salter leaned against the shelves. He had only two questions to ask. "Why you?" was the first. "Why are they threatening a bookstore?"

She raised her hands in dismay. "I don't know why me. I don't even care that much. None of the peddlers sells children's books and my customers couldn't care less about any garbage. I mean the kids."

"You haven't been a spokesman on this issue."

"I haven't even been to the meetings. I feel a bit of a radical about it all, and anyway, getting the people around here to act like a group—well, it just isn't what they are about. I once tried to get a petition to get the city to repair the sidewalk—that minefield out there breaks two ankles and four pairs of glasses a year, take a look when you go out—it's been like that for ten years. But when I went around to get people to sign up, it was like pulling hens' teeth. They tend not to be joiners, as long as they're making money."

"If it doesn't make any sense, then would any of the traders have anything personal against you, all five of you?"

"Not that I know of. I've never spoken to them as individuals, except to buy the odd thing. I've never spoken against then, either, or for them." She spoke brightly, with the slightly affected jauntiness that Salter now associated with a private school background.

The door behind them opened and banged into Salter. He moved aside to let in a man dressed in a blue linen suit and a darker blue open-necked shirt. His hair was gray but thick and elegant, the hair of a man of distinction. His face had deep concertina folds along the cheeks and numerous small creases elsewhere like an old leather bag that has been crushed. When he smiled, the folds of his face became so deep that Salter wondered how he shaved.

Ruth Pearson stood up and now the three of them were face-to-face and only inches apart. "This is David Leese, Inspector," she said. "And this is Inspector Salter. He's inquiring about the threatening letters."

The two men shook hands and maneuvered around each other so that Leese could pass by him. Salter stood in the doorway. "You work here, Mr. Leese?" he asked.

"Just on Saturdays, to help Ruth."

"He's a friend," Ruth said.

"What about Nystrom? Does he work here? Should I talk to him?"

She nodded. "Another friend. Talk to him by all means. David will look after the cash now."

But at that moment Nystrom called "Ruthie" from the front of the store, in a yoo-hooing voice. "I have to go. I'm trying to sell my house on Admiral. I must be there by eleven."

Ruth Pearson looked at Salter to see if he wanted Nystrom detained. Understanding, he shook his head. "I'll come back. Selling your house is important stuff."

"Oh, it's not *his* house. He's in real estate. Well, it is his house, but that's what he does. He buys old houses and refurbishes them and sells them."

They walked to the front of the store where Leese was already tending the cash register. "Sorry I'm not more help," she said. "You might try Vera. The dress shop a couple of doors down."

Salter looked at the piece of paper he took from his pocket. "I've talked to her already," he said.

"And she's talked to *you*," Nystrom said, and they all laughed.

The owners of the restaurant and the luggage shop were waiting for Salter. They had been talking to each other and they wanted a twenty-four-hour guard on their premises. "You've already got one," Salter said. "We posted a round-the-clock watch on these stores when the second letters came in."

The jeweler had made his own arrangements: He had hired a private security guard and locked his door. Customers had to present themselves for scrutiny before they were admitted. "I might as well have stayed in Detroit," he said.

"None of this is necessary. We're looking after the stores."

"You don't think so? *You* didn't get the letters. Have you found out who wrote them? When you do, I'll unlock the door."

Vera was the most disturbed by the second letter, but her response was different. Instead of the aggressive, demanding attitude she had taken up in the first interview, she now pulled Salter closer, seeking protection. "Who do you think it is?" she asked immediately, holding his arm and looking into his face. "They sound like a load of terrorists, don't they? I was thinking of closing up for a few weeks. Do you think I should?"

"No, I don't." Salter shook himself free and stepped back a pace. "We've got a guard on the store."

But she wasn't really asking his advice, just talking to herself, fearfully. "I could go back to London for a couple of weeks, stay with my sister, I suppose."

"It's probably a scare tactic. They just want you to stop complaining about them."

"Yes, but *two* letters! You can't tell, can you? Some of these immigrants are quite used to setting off bombs, aren't they? I could get that wire-mesh stuff, I suppose. I don't know. Do your men know how to handle things like this? I mean, you haven't had much experience with this kind of thing in Canada, have you? I'm not letting anyone leave any parcels in my shop."

"Look," Salter said, noisily. "Don't get in a panic. We've got it under control. Now, let me ask you once more. Have you any idea who might be behind it? Among the street traders, that is."

"Oh, no, no. How would I know? I was just making a general complaint, that's all. Oh, no, I can't imagine who it could be."

I don't want to get involved, Salter thought. Aloud, he said, "Let me know if you get any ideas," and left her shaking her head.

From Vera's he took one more look at the street traders on Bloor Street, then returned to the Coffee Mill where two detectives were waiting for him. They had been in the area since early morning, questioning the peddlers as they arrived to take up their stands.

"Nothing," one of the detectives said. "Not a thing. They don't know nothing and they haven't heard nothing and nobody's acting like he's lying. Right, Sid?"

The other detective nodded. "You think it's serious?" he asked Salter. "I mean, threatening letters. It happens. It's usually someone getting his rocks off. They don't follow up."

"I know. But the Princess is coming."

"That's right." The detective looked mock solemn. "I nearly forgot. Well, if you don't need us anymore, our staff sergeant wants us back home. He's got his own stuff for us to do."

"Go ahead. Thanks."

As the two detectives stood up, one of them nodded at the check. "They know you here?" he asked.

Salter picked up the check and put it with his own. "Yeah," he said. "But don't charge anything to my account, will you."

After they had gone, he stayed for another cup of coffee until he had decided what to do next, then paid the bill, leaving a large tip. He had an idea that he would be seeing a lot of this place in the next two weeks.

He spent the rest of the afternoon in the area. The tourists were arriving for the weekend and it was easy for him to mix with the crowds and shuffle along Bloor Street from Bellair to Yonge, stopping to window-shop at every trader along the curb. When a uniformed constable gave one of the traders a ticket for obstructing traffic, he was close enough to be able to commiserate.

"That could get expensive," he said, nodding to the ticket still in the man's hand.

"One a day is rent. Four a day I can't handle," the man said.

"They go that high?"

"Some days. When the merchants are feeling nasty." The man broke off to attend to a customer, and Salter moved on.

By the end of the afternoon he had confirmed that if the traders were linked in a conspiracy he wouldn't find out about it this way, but he had also formed a powerful conviction that the whole idea was very unlikely. Nevertheless, he reported to Orliff that he would have a recommendation for him on Monday, before the meeting, and went home to think about it.

WHEN HE pulled into his driveway, he saw Seth's bike propped against the house and wondered how the boy's relationship with his grandfather was developing. Once he had his jacket off and a beer in his hand, he called his father to give him a chance to raise the subject. The old man answered immediately. He was very angry.

"What's the bloody idea?" he shouted. "Sending a goddamn social worker to see me. I spent half the goddamn afternoon getting rid of her. Practically forced her way in, she did, then started nosing around the place until I told her to piss off. She said she'd been asked to call by a member of the family. There's only you, so what's the bloody idea?"

It was rare for the old man to swear when he was at home, a sign that he was very upset.

"I didn't send any social worker round, Dad. It must have been a mistake. If she comes back, don't let her in."

"No fear of that. I won't be caught a second time. But how did she come to see me if you didn't send her? She had the name right."

"Some computer mistake probably. Don't let her in next time."

"I don't *have* to let her in, do I?"

"No. Tell her no one gets in without a warrant."

"Right. I don't have to tell her what we eat, either, do I? She stuck this goddamn nutritional chart on the fridge door, but I had it off as soon as she left."

"You don't have to tell her anything. Okay?"

"Right. I was a bit careful because I thought she might be trying to find out about me and May."

Now Salter realized that because of his live-in relation-ship with May, his father felt vulnerable to official snoops. He had lived all his life knowing that the kind of arrange-ment he had was immoral and he wasn't absolutely cer-tain that it wasn't illegal, too.

"What's May got to do with it?" Salter asked.

"I don't know, do I? They could see there's just the one bedroom. I've been trying to figure it out. If I was on wel-fare or like that, I'd have to put up with them walking in and out when they felt like it, but none of that applies. I mean, even if you did send her round, I don't have to let her in, do I?"

"No, Dad, you don't have to let her in."

"Right, then. Even if you did send her I can still tell her to get stuffed, can't I? May and I are nobody's business. Right?"

"Right. And I didn't send her round."

"Somebody did." The old man hung up.

Salter called up the stairs. "Seth!" When the boy ap-peared, he asked him, "Did you send a social worker to see Grandfather?"

"Yes, I did. There's a pamphlet in the library which tells about all the services available to senior citizens, but I knew he wouldn't use any of them unless someone talked him into it, so I found out who to phone and told them how lonely he was."

"Let's go over it again. In the first place, he's not lonely. He's got May."

"But she never says anything. He *must* be lonely."

"He isn't. Okay? Second, he's not old. Other people are old, not him. Old is, like, ninety as far as he's concerned. He's only seventy-three or four. So he feels insulted if someone calls him a poor old man. Last, he doesn't like social workers."

"What's the matter with social workers?"

"He doesn't like them because once upon a time when he was a kid to have the equivalent of a social worker call on you was a disgrace. Grandfather's proud, see, and if a social worker calls on him he thinks it's because the neighbors have complained that he doesn't wash anymore. Who knows what goes on inside his head? So leave him alone."

Seth looked mutinous. "I'm still going to see him."

"Fine. Call first, though. He's not used to a lot of attention. He doesn't understand it. And don't try to hug him."

ON MONDAY AFTERNOON there was a meeting in the deputy chief's office. Salter talked to Orliff early in the morning. "I need an undercover man, someone to pose as a street trader. I still don't think there's anything going on with them, but if there is, we might be able to overhear something."

"I don't think I can get you anyone. Everybody's screaming about the extra workload now."

Salter shrugged. "Okay. We've got a watch on the stores. We've gone round the traders. I've talked to the owners. I don't know what else to do. If we don't find out what's behind these letters, and they *are* serious . . ."

"Okay, okay. It's too obvious, isn't it? If they could rain a little on her parade, it would be very good publicity. Okay, I'll see what I can do. Stay in your office. I'll call around."

An hour later there was a knock on Salter's door and a young man entered, thin and dark, with black curly hair almost to his shoulders, wearing creased white pants and a black cotton sweater. "Inspector Salter?" Receiving confirmation, he came in and closed the door behind him. "Ranovic," he said.

"Is that the password?"

"No, it's me. Ranovic."

It was difficult to tell anything from the man's bearing. He acted like someone in a disco striking up a conversation with a stranger. Salter waited for more.

The man straightened up. "Constable Ranovic, sir, reporting for duty."

"The undercover guy? Right. Sit down."

Ranovic smiled, recovering his opening poise, and sat down facing Salter. "What's the detail, sir?"

Salter explained.

Ranovic laughed. "Street trader. That's great. What'll I sell? Not hot dogs, please."

"Got any ideas?"

Ranovic gave it a moment's thought. "Buttons. Postcards. Stuff like that. Union Jacks."

"Where will you get your merchandise?"

"No sweat. I know a guy. I'll get one of those boards on a stick. Be more mobile. Money?"

"Find out what you need to set up. I'll give you a voucher to draw what you need."

"I'll need a license."

"I'll fix that now." Salter took a card from his wallet and picked up the telephone. "Councillor Fitch," he said when he was through to City Hall. When Fitch responded he explained what he wanted. "That's Metro," Fitch said. "I'm City."

"If I have to go up the line, it'll take too long."

"I'll call you back."

Salter put the phone down and turned back to Ranovic. "Concentrate on the section of Bloor Street between Bellair and Bay. If you think it's smart, go as far as Yonge

Street. Get in among them. Report in by phone twice a day.''

"Sometimes it's good to have a face-to-face. Meet somewhere safe.''

"If that happens, we can find somewhere. Maybe we could meet on the ferry going to the islands. I could drop something and you could pick it up. Very natural. I saw them do that in a TV show.''

"We don't have to do all that," Ranovic protested. "We could just . . . oh, you're kidding, right?''

"Sorry. What's your regular detail?''

"I'm on the drug squad. Same kind of thing. Under-cover.''

"Is there any chance someone will recognize you on Bloor Street?''

"Not much. I deal out in the West End. The Simcoe Hotel, nearly out to Mississauga. They don't come into town much.''

"You *deal*?''

"Sure. That's my cover. I buy dope from a supplier we're after at the Simcoe Hotel. He thinks I sell it retail.''

The phone rang. It was Fitch. "Got it," he said. "Norbert Lunn is looking after it. Now who is it for?''

"What's your first name?" Salter asked Ranovic, covering the mouthpiece.

"Gorgi. Gorgi Ranovic.''

"Gorgi Ranovic," Salter repeated into the phone.

Ranovic waved at him excitedly. "Tell him to make it out to Bruno Caroli," he whispered.

"Why?''

"That's my cover. I pass as Italian.''

"Why?''

"The mob has access to the police nominal roll, see.''

"Everybody has access to the nominal roll. If you want to know if someone is on the force you can just call Public Affairs."

"That's why I have to have a name that isn't on the list, see?"

"But...oh, for Pete's sake. All right." He uncovered the mouthpiece. "Make out the license to Bruno Caroli. He'll pick it up this afternoon. Thanks. And tell the Metro guy thanks, too." He put the phone down. "So you're in business. When can you get on the street?"

"I'll be there tomorrow. Drive along Bloor, you'll see me. Don't wave, though." Ranovic grinned. "I'll call in tomorrow afternoon."

Salter scribbled a voucher for the funds Ranovic needed. The constable tucked it away in a baggy side pocket, saying, "Wish me luck," raised an open hand in a slightly too familiar salute, and left.

IN THE DEPUTY'S OFFICE that afternoon, Salter listened to the complex arrangements that were being cemented in place for the visit. When his turn came, he reported on his failure to find the sender of the anonymous letters. Before he could outline what he had planned, he was interrupted from the other end of the table.

"Let's sweep the whole area," Sergeant Crawley said. "Just in case." Crawley had been assigned a small tactical squad to be parked on a side street one block away from the route the Princess was to take. He thought of himself as in charge of a kind of S.A.S. unit, and he used words like "sweep" and "strike" and "clear zone" to show how he saw himself.

Hancock, the staff superintendent in charge of Metro's share of security, said, "Sweep? Who? Where? When?"

"Go in early on Saturday. Take out the traders and the rest of the bums."

"What about the ones who arrive after sunup?" Salter asked. Down the table someone snickered.

"Huh?" Crawley inquired.

"I think Salter means we can't keep the traders out of the whole area," Hancock said. "We can keep them off the route, of course, but they have the right to be in the area. We'll just have to watch them. That's Salter's job."

Salter said, "I'd like four men posted on the day to keep the peddlers from coming in down the side streets."

"Has Gorgi Ranovic reported in yet?" Orliff asked.

"Who the hell is Georgy-Porgy?" Crawley wanted to know.

"Just Gorgi. With an 'i'. Gorgi Ranovic. Yes, he has." Salter turned to face Crawley. "He's working for us undercover. We borrowed him from the drug squad. He's going to be selling souvenir buttons and postcards, so if you have to make a strike or a roll-back, keep your eyes open for a thin, dark-haired guy selling pictures of the CN tower. He's one of ours."

Hancock signaled the end of the meeting, and Salter went back to his office.

For the next week, Ranovic called in regularly with nothing to report, and by the weekend Salter had so relaxed about the threats that he decided to take the opportunity of the lull to drive up to Stoney Lake and look for art forgers. He dug out his fishing tackle, Annie packed him some sandwiches, and early on Monday morning he set out for the lake.

FIVE

HE ARRIVED at the landing at ten-thirty and rented a small aluminum boat with a ten-horsepower motor. He showed the operator of the marina the photograph of the painting. "I want to take a picture of the church from the same angle," he explained. "See how close the painting is to the real thing."

The operator didn't question him, but called to an Indian helper on the dock. "Hector knows the lake backwards," he said.

Hector looked at the picture, then slowly moved himself through ninety degrees, looking alternately at the lake and the picture. "Near the Argyles' place," he pronounced.

"Where's that?"

Hector explained, pointing out the channel and listing the landmarks to watch for, and Salter set off.

It was a quiet time of the week, still at the beginning of the season, and except for a houseboat lumbering through the waterway, Salter had that part of the lake to himself. It took him half an hour to find the spot Hector had located and to confirm the view he was looking for. He got out his rod and trolled the shoreline within the limits of the view, and established that the painting must have been done within a range of about two hundred yards; outside this, the church disappeared. He made notes about the cottages that lay within the range and returned to the marina in the middle of the afternoon. There, after a lot of false starts, he managed to get Hector chatting about the

owners around the lake and who among them were paint-
ers. If it wasn't an owner, he would have to find out if
anyone had rented a cottage to a painter. Hector responded immediately. "There's only one," he said. "Jack
Colbert. Flies one of those itsy-bitsy planes round the lake.
He's the only painter I know of. He's not where you were,
though. The Colberts' place is a mile up the lake, around
the bend."

Salter asked him to confine himself to the cottages in the
area he had been fishing. Did any of their owners paint?
He saw the answer on Hector's face as he tried to be helpful. "I expect some of them do," he said. "The ladies,
probably."

"But you haven't seen them. Actually set up outside, I
mean. On the rocks. Painting."

"Not this year, no."

"Last year? The year before?"

"No."

"Can you tell me who owns these cottages?"

"Sure." Hector listed them off.

"Do you have their addresses?"

"Ellard does. Come on inside. I'll get them for you." He
led the way into the marina building, and took down a
small wooden box from a back shelf behind the counter.
The box contained a card index of owners who main-
tained charge accounts at the marina, and Salter copied
down the ones he was interested in. They were all Toronto
addresses.

It was almost time for supper, and Salter reserved a boat
for the next day and went in search of a motel and a diner.
That evening, after supper, he watched a rerun of a Sher-
lock Holmes episode on television. As he was sliding toward sleep, the solution to his own problem came to him.
Amis Settle wasn't dead. He had simply moved to Paris (or

better yet, Tahiti), where he had staged his own death. Eventually, haunted by his boyhood memories, he had returned to Canada and Stoney Lake, where no one recognized him, married an Indian woman, and begun painting again in his old style. The picture was genuine, and Salter would eventually get the truth from Hector, the marina helper, who was Amis Settle's grandson. Salter had read the story a hundred times.

HE WAS AWAKENED the next morning by an Ontario Provincial Police constable banging on the door of the motel unit. He had a message from Orliff: Ranovic was concerned about something. Salter scrounged a cup of coffee from the marina operator as he canceled the boat and drove reluctantly back to Toronto, leaving behind a lake shining with the promise of a wonderful day to do some investigating with a fishing rod.

At the office he found four messages from Ranovic, who had been trying to get him since Monday afternoon. He waited for another message until five o'clock, then left a message of his own that Ranovic was to call him at home after seven.

THE PHONE RANG three times after dinner. The first time a girl calling herself Debbie offered him a special on carpet cleaning. The second caller told him he had been selected to receive a hundred dollars' worth of free gifts. All he had to do was answer a few questions. He disposed of both of these with minimum courtesy, not for the first time looking forward to the technology which would allow him to see who was calling before he had to answer. The third call was from his father.

"Tell that kid to stop it," his father said as soon as he heard Salter's voice. "That goddamn mailman brings me a stack of brochures every morning and the kid comes by every afternoon with another pile. I had the local minister around today, sent by him. Tell him to stop it. I know he means well, but he's driving me crazy.''

Salter laughed. His father had a deep distrust of all clergymen. In the working-class Anglican way, he never went near a church except for marriages and deaths, and these days such ceremonies often took place elsewhere. Having experienced no spiritual hankerings himself, he found such matters awkward to think about. Clergymen, for him, were a blighted lot who wished to blight all others. "What are the brochures about?'' Salter asked.

"Everything,'' the old man said. "Everything to do with being bloody old. How you can travel around the world with a lot of old farts; old games and handicrafts they go in for at the community center. You name it, they've thought of a way old people can do it. One thing for sure, there must be a lot of money in the old. Must be. But tell him to lay off, will you? May and I have got the TV, Greenwood racetrack most nights, and sometimes we go across the hall for a hand of euchre. Tell him we're too busy for all this stuff, will you.'' He hung up before Salter could try to soothe him.

After that there was silence for an hour while Salter watched television, waiting for Ranovic to call. At nine o'clock there was a knock at the door. Annie answered it and called Salter. Ranovic was standing on the porch.

"Your phone is off the hook,'' he said.

Salter motioned Ranovic into the front room, away from the television, and picked up the telephone. Angus was in the middle of explaining to his girlfriend how to write an essay.

"It might as well be,'' he said. "How did you know where I live?'''

"I got it from the office. I live on Balliol so I figured it was easier to drive over than keep trying to get through. I was calling for about two hours."

"Sorry." They were almost even. His irritation at Ranovic for invading his private life was matched by Ranovic's wasted evening. "So what's happened?"

But Ranovic was staring around him. "This is nice," he said. "Did you fix it up yourself?"

It was the classic question about the last remodeling Annie had put the house through. "We had it done."

"Yeah? It's nice. How long have you lived here?"

"Twenty years."

"Is *that right*?" Ranovic's tone gave Salter credit for a remarkable performance, as if he had balanced on one leg the whole time. "You have a family?"

"I have two boys, seventeen and fourteen. That was my wife who let you in. And there's the cat."

But Ranovic wasn't finished. "Is *that right*?" he said again. "Your wife's very young looking for a mature lady."

"For forty-three she's still pretty nimble," Salter agreed. "Now what's happening?"

Ranovic shook his head several times and returned to business.

"You want a drink before we get into it?" Salter asked.

"How do you mean?"

Jesus. Somebody in his life must have asked him that before. "You want a drink? Scotch, gin, beer, wine? Whatever. I'm going to have a Scotch. How about you?"

"Oh, no. I don't drink hard stuff. It destroys your entire waste disposal system. I'll have a beer."

Salter went to fetch the drinks, leaving Ranovic to walk around the room, admiring its wonders. When he returned, he brought an ashtray with him. "None of us smoke," he said. "But you can if you want."

"Cigarettes? Oh, no."

Salter began to wonder if Ranovic's cover was deep enough to conceal a Seventh-Day Adventist. He tried to probe. "You can't smoke dope here if that's what you're wondering. I'm hoping my kids will bypass it."

Ranovic nodded his approval. "Sure. I wouldn't smoke up in a family-type place."

"Good. Now let's get on."

"Right. I called you because I think there's something going on. Just a feeling, but there's a lot of private stuff happening, whispering, like in one of those convict movies just before the jailbreak. When I come near them, they stop."

"How many of them? Can you nail it down to individuals?"

"Nah. I can't tell who's doing the instigating or even who's in on it. Right now they seem to be talking it up among themselves, maybe getting each other involved. I can't tell yet."

"But you think it's something to do with the visit?"

"Somebody's planning something. The visit is the most likely."

Maybe Sergeant Crawley was right. If there really was a plan for a major demonstration, enough to interfere with security, then the only safe thing would be to pick up the traders as they arrived on Saturday morning and take them fifty miles away for questioning, bringing them back when the walkabout was over. It was standard procedure for potentially disruptive elements. But perhaps because it was Crawley's idea, Salter was reluctant to agree with it if there was any other way.

"If there are a lot of them involved, it can't be dangerous, just a nuisance," he said. "Anyone planning anything really nasty wouldn't be talking it up. And someone would have told us. Those traders don't look rough to me."

"They aren't. Peaceniks, some of them."

"Can you find out what's happening in the next two days?"

"I don't know. See, it's like any other job. I need time to get them to trust me. I should just sit still for a few weeks and let them come to me."

"We haven't got a few weeks. Do they suspect you? Of being a cop?"

"No way." Ranovic was shocked. "No, it's just that I'm new on the street, see. Let me try something. I'll call you tomorrow afternoon, and if I'm not getting anywhere you can do what you have to."

Annie appeared in the doorway. Ranovic jumped to his feet and Salter introduced him. "You have a very nice home," the constable told her.

"Thank you. Would you like some coffee? I'm just making some for us."

Ranovic looked embarrassed, and Salter wondered what the trouble was. "We're having some," he repeated.

"No, thanks, sir. I don't drink coffee, stuff like that."

Stuff like what? Drano? Bleach? Paint thinner? "Another beer, then?" Salter asked.

"Nah, I'd better go. Nice to meet you, Mrs. Salter."

At the door, just before Ranovic left, Salter asked, "Why don't you drink coffee?" He had to know.

"It screws up your chemical balance. My girlfriend's into homeopathy, and there's lots of stuff we don't take now."

Is that right? Salter closed the door, feeling like a walking sack of poison, then went to the front window to watch Ranovic pause on the sidewalk and survey the house for a full minute before he got into his car and drove off.

RANOVIC CALLED the next afternoon to report success. Gambling that he was right, that the activity he had been observing concerned the walkabout, he had decided to try to smoke out the plan by announcing one of his own. During the morning he had approached three or four of the traders who seemed most involved in the conversations with a scheme of his own to create some publicity for their cause by staging a demonstration during the royal visit. Ranovic wanted to know who would go along with him. It worked. At noon he was approached in return by two of the traders who asked him to drop his idea and join up with them. Five or six of them were planning to demonstrate on Hazelton Avenue, outside the Lanes, right after the parade. They weren't going to interrupt the parade itself, just take advantage of the crowds.

"So that's it," Ranovic said. "They're harmless. I'm going along with them, of course. I'll stay in touch. Kind of fun, this."

"You don't think there's a problem, then?"

"There's no problem. None at all. Tell your boys to quit worrying about the traders. We're harmless."

But Salter had to get approval and cover himself, so at the Friday morning meeting he reported the situation. "All we need is a uniformed man outside Hazelton Lanes who knows what it's all about. If we keep them away until the walkabout is over, then they can still have themselves a little protest."

"I still think we should sweep them off the streets," Crawley said. "I don't trust those goddamn hippies."

"These people aren't hippies, for God's sake. You're twenty years out of date," Salter said.

Crawley's face bulged, but the staff superintendent cut him off. "All right, Salter. But stay on top of it."

"I don't see any problem, sir. If they do get silly, we'll have a lot of help from the crowd control people. We can let them know what to expect, just in case."

II

———————————————————

SIX

AT ONE MINUTE after the hour, two gold-braided door-men pulled open the doors of the Park Plaza Hotel and the Princess walked out, accompanied by a tall, thin lady in a large hat, the mayor, and several tall, thick bodyguards whose job it was to make sure that while the Princess was in motion no one else came within fifty feet of her.

The crowd on the sidewalk clapped as she appeared; even after hours of waiting they responded noisily to the famous shy smile under the wide straw hat.

"She's just like her pictures," one of the spectators, a middle-aged woman with a slight Scandinavian accent, said. "Not a lot of makeup, has she, Helga? I thought they wore tons of it. In public, I mean."

"No, no," Helga said. "No, no. Not these ones. They don't need much makeup. They are naturally red in the face. The English, I mean. Hooray," she added as the Princess passed. "Hooray, Your Highness."

"That lady is beautiful," the first woman said with some violence. "Beautiful," she repeated, clapping hard and staring around for signs of disagreement.

A row of Toronto's finest formed a guard across Avenue Road. Behind them, several layers of security forces watched the crowd as it pressed closer. A few extremely young citizens with their parents, as well as some very old people, were allowed in the front row, but most of the first two rows were made up of various kinds of guards.

The Queen's Plate, the oldest continually run stakes race in North America, is traditionally graced by the presence of one of the royals. The Princess had arrived on Friday in time to attend the obligatory banquet of politicians and their wives in the evening. On Saturday morning she visited a Bloor Street store that was having an exhibition of British china in honor of her visit, made the usual journey to the top of the CN tower (the tallest free-standing "structure" in the world), and lunched with a few dozen of the Toronto establishment in the rooftop restaurant of the Park Plaza. Now she was ready to open the first annual Yorkville Festival.

A helicopter passed over the heads of the crowd that pressed forward against the police as the Princess reached the far curb. The security operation involved the police of three forces: the R.C.M.P., the Ontario Provincial Police, and the Metropolitan Police. The Princess had also brought her own security force with her, so, apart from the police assigned to crowd control, the security arrangements involved several hundred Canadians and half a dozen Englishmen. Some friction had already developed between the Canadians, determined to protect the country's reputation for safety, and the Princess's own bodyguards, who saw themselves as the experts because they looked after her for three hundred and sixty-five days a year. No matter what arrangements the Canadians made, the chief of the English bodyguards intended to respond to any emergency as he saw fit, a point he had already made clear to a commander of the R.C.M.P. and several Metro superintendents. The members of her guard stood next to her at all times; her chief bodyguard had brought with him the badges to be worn by the security forces, and issued them, himself, at the very last moment. The badges, necessary for the security men to recognize one another, were simple white disks, the size of a quarter, in three grades: Those with a red polka dot in the center were assigned to forces that swept the buildings along the route, moved among the crowds, and formed the surveillance wall immediately behind the uniformed police; they did not approach the royal party unless specifically ordered. Those wearing the badges with a blue dot formed a second, inner ring; they rode in the lead cars and sat in adjoining boxes at the racetrack. Only wearers of the black dot, all of them vetted by the Princess's bodyguards, could physically approach the royal party. The bodyguards wore no badges.

The Princess crossed the sidewalk and cut the ribbon, declaring the festival well and truly open, and the party began its progress past the luxury hotel and condominium which flanked the entrance to Cumberland Avenue.

The visit to Yorkville was planned to take half an hour. Down Cumberland to Bellair, along Bellair to the old jail (now a lockup for antiques), then west along Yorkville to Avenue Road, where a fleet of cars waited to drive the royal party to Woodbine racetrack.

Once more the helicopter passed overhead, searching the crowd.

"For what?" the pilot wanted to know. He and his helicopter were from the Ministry of the Environment, pressed into extraordinary service. Usually he looked for forest fires from much higher up.

"Someone on a roof with a gun," the sergeant said, not looking at him.

"Then what? You got orders to shoot to kill?"

The sergeant, wearing a red dot, looked sideways at the pilot, who was wearing his khaki uniform and a tie for the occasion. "In the event of an emergency," the sergeant said, "I have this envelope taped to my forearm which I then proceed to unseal, read the enclosed instructions, and act accordingly. Then you'll know, too."

"You *what*?" the pilot squawked. "You have to open a goddamn *envelope*? And . . ." His voice ran out of power as he realized he had been had. "Yeah, well. Make sure you're facing the right way when you pull the fucking trigger, eh," he concluded.

"Go back along the same sweep. I want to see what's behind that vent," the sergeant said. "And shut up." He looked down at the party of dignitaries strolling along Bellair in a bubble of calm carved by the police out of the seething crowds packing the street. Beyond the crowds, traffic was stopped for dozens of blocks around, nearly to the edge of his field of vision. University Avenue and Bloor Street west of University had been blocked off and were backed up for miles. Bloor Street east of University was filled with people trying to get through to the action in the village. North of Bloor, Avenue Road was clear of traffic and lined with barricades holding back the crowds waiting to see the Princess on her way to the racetrack.

The Princess's party had now reached Yorkville Avenue and waited as she paused to exclaim at something in the window of the antique store before continuing down the street to the waiting cars.

INSIDE THE TRUCK parked in the basement of the garage farther down Yorkville, the girl heard the crowd telling itself that the Princess was coming, and shifted from a sitting position to squatting on her haunches for what she hoped was the last time. The operation had been carefully planned; every detail had been thought of except the girl's comfort. She had been inside the truck now for five hours with only two chocolate bars and nothing to drink. The floor of the Chevrolet van was ridged and studded with bolts, and the girl had only the thin cloth which had concealed her when they searched the van, not even a jacket to wad into a cushion. For the last hour she had been desperately in need of a pee, but there was no relief possible inside the van. There was an old antifreeze container—a plastic, log-shaped bottle with a neck opening that would have served perfectly for a man in her circumstances—and the girl tried to distract herself by composing an essay in her head about how this was one more example of the fact that the world was made for and by men. She was not squeamish, but she had no idea of what would happen if she peed on the floor; her mind leaped to images of sharp-eyed guards pointing to her trail as it emerged shyly from under the van.

Fifteen minutes. She stretched herself out on the floor of the van, knowing she would be able to stand the ridges digging into her back for about two minutes, but taking a few seconds' pleasure from being able to stretch. The essential thing was to flex all of her muscles and joints continuously, to keep herself loose in the starting blocks. She would have a minute, and the use of one hand, to slide back the door of the van, run, doubled over, using the van as cover, crossing to the stair exit, up half a flight of stairs and out onto Yorkville as the Princess arrived. Incredibly, lying there, her spine pressed against the hard iron, her bladder begging for relief, she felt drowsy and forced herself to sit up. She tried to fill her mind with a distracting concern. What, she wondered, are the techniques for creating tension, avoiding sleep? She knew how to induce sleep by relaxing each muscle one at a time, starting with her toes. But was there a way to make your toes tense?

Two stories above her, on the roof of the Stuart Jackson Gallery, Charlie Salter was looking down Hazelton Avenue, watching a small group of people assemble. He saw that they were far enough away to be no threat to the walkabout, and he went back to daydreaming and looking in the crowds for his wife, who had promised to wave to him.

His walkie-talkie crackled.

"Inspector? Ranovic here. We're on Hazelton."

"I can see you. She's nearly passed this end now, so they can't upset anything."

"Something's going on down at your end. These people are excited about something. Watch the garage, they keep saying. The one opposite Hazelton, they mean."

"Watch it? What for?"

"I don't know. I'm just passing it on. Watch the garage."

"What's that gang doing now?"

"We're going to have a little protest after she's gone."

"I can see four of you. That right?"

"Five counting me. We're going to try and get on TV."

"Right." Salter ran down the ladder and out through the gallery to the garage, which had an exit on Yorkville. It was closed tight until the Princess was well clear, the door guarded by a uniformed policeman. Salter pointed to his red dot and was let in through the side door.

"When was this place checked?" he asked.

"Nine o'clock. When we closed it up."

"You check every car and truck?"

"Sure. Looked underneath every one, too. The whole bit."

"Find anything?"

The policeman shook his head. "There was one kid, hiding in one of those hippie vans, in the basement. Said he was hoping to see the Princess from in here. We sent him on his way."

"Show me."

The van was parked about fifty feet from the wall in the corner of the basement. It was hand-painted with grotesques on the sides—dragonflies with human torsos, centaurs with the hindquarters of lizards.

"Did he kick up a fuss, this kid?"

"No, he just took off somewhere. He went out of here reading a book."

Through the open sides of the garage, the noise of the royal party's approach increased to a roar. Salter ran over to the van and listened by the side door. After a minute he pulled the door open. "Don't get up," he said. "Just sit there until I tell you to move. It won't be long now."

The girl squinted at him and stayed sitting cross-legged on the floor of the van. Beside her, a hand sign bore the slogan "Yorkville Street Traders Beg Your Majesty's Help."

"What did you plan to do, throw yourself in front of her?"

Outside, the crowd applauded as the Princess reached the door of the garage. "That's exactly what I'm going to do," the girl said, scrambling to her feet and launching herself at the open door.

Gently, Salter pushed her back. "I'll lock you up if you get too antsy," he said.

Now the cheering was dying as the Princess passed on her way. There were no pauses planned for the last fifty yards of the Princess's walk, Salter knew. The girl crouched on the floor of the van, still holding her sign.

"Couple of minutes," Salter said. "Then you can go."

"Aren't you going to arrest me?"

"What for? You'll find your pals on Hazelton Avenue, by the way. They were watching for you, like me." He cocked an ear to the noises from the street. The Princess, he estimated, had now reached the car that was waiting to take her to the racetrack.

A policeman appeared in the stairwell leading to the street. "We've got orders to open up as soon as she's gone by," he said.

"Okay. Go ahead. There's no problem here."

The policeman disappeared, and a few minutes later the first cars appeared on the ramp. They parked quickly and the drivers ran upstairs, hoping to catch a last glimpse of the Princess.

"You can go now," Salter said to the girl.

She was in her early twenties, Salter guessed, with a chunky figure dressed in a white T-shirt and a long denim skirt. She seemed unintimidated by Salter and the constable. When they stood back, she climbed down and walked off toward the stairs, moving in long strides with her head thrust forward.

"By the way," he called after her, "she's not a 'majesty.' She's a 'highness.' That's what we were told to call her."

The girl turned her face to him and he wondered what she would call him (his favorite was "snot-gobbling fuck-pig," which he had once been called by a boy of twelve when he was dealing with a domestic disturbance on Gerrard Street). But this girl did not deal in easy obscenities. "Nobody told me," she said. "And I don't have my crayons with me. Think she'll understand?"

Salter laughed as his radio beeped. "What happened?" Constable Ranovic wanted to know.

"Nothing," Salter said. "We caught her before she could make a fuss. She was going to wave a placard under Her Highness's nose. What's happening with you?"

"We are just forming up to march round the village, take advantage of the crowds to get our message across. Can I go now?"

"No. Stay with them until they disperse, in case they get silly. Maybe they've got something else planned."

"Okay. But I think it's all over. Here we go."

SALTER'S JOB WAS OVER, too. By now the Princess was halfway to the races, and he decided to treat himself to a cheese Danish in a restaurant on Cumberland, then realized it was no day for a quiet coffee in the village: Every café and restaurant would be jammed for another hour. He stepped out of the crowd on the sidewalk, wondering whether to go home or back to headquarters to write up his report. His mind was made up for him by the realization that he was having his pocket picked, clumsily, and he grabbed the wrist and hauled the pickpocket around in front of him. "Hi, Charlie," Annie said. "I thought I might find you here."

"Did you see her?" he asked.

"Mmmm. She looked..."

"I know. *Lovely*. You got the car?"

"It's behind the hotel. You finished now?"

"Yeah, she's safe. England can sleep peacefully. Let's go home and watch the big race on television. That way I might get to see her, too."

They started to make their way toward Avenue Road, to the parking lot behind the Park Plaza Hotel. Then Salter grabbed Annie's arm and turned them onto Old York Lane. "I want to have a quick look at that gang on Hazelton," he said.

"You'll miss the race."

"Can you get the car? I'll meet you in ten minutes, at the end of Webster."

She nodded and disappeared. Salter walked down Hazelton Avenue past Hazelton Lanes and found the little group of protesters still being gently but very firmly kept back from the crowds. The girl from the van was with them now, and she was arguing with a sergeant who was preventing them from coming south. Salter entertained himself by watching Ranovic, in his white trousers and black sweater, waving his banner with the rest of them, leading them on in a way, because the others looked more self-conscious than he, as if they were new to the protesting scene. As Salter watched, the sergeant put his radio away and made a gesture indicating they were free to march. Ranovic spotted Salter watching him from across the street. "Yay, yay," Ranovic shouted. "Yorkville unfair to street traders." The girl from the van took up his shout and the others followed along, trying to make a unified chant of it. As they passed Salter, Ranovic gave his placard an extra twiddle. "No more police harassment," he shouted. The girl from the van saw Salter and tossed her head, something Salter had never actually seen done before. He turned and walked back to Avenue Road.

Annie was waiting for him on the corner of Webster Avenue. "Finished?" she asked as he climbed into the car.

"All wrapped up. All I had to do was make sure those street traders didn't do anything dumb. Now I can put my feet up for the weekend."

Avenue Road was still crowded with people who had gathered to watch the Princess pass by. Charlie and Annie got home just in time to pour the beer and settle down in front of the television screen before the Princess arrived at the track.

"Here she comes," Annie said.

They watched the landau, surrounded by outriders, make its way down the track and stop opposite the stands. As the Princess descended and began shaking the hands of Toronto's sportsmen, Salter entertained himself by identifying the security forces in her entourage. The horse-drawn carriage had been preceded by a limousine and succeeded by two more, all packed full of guards, giving the impression (apart from the carriage) that either a gangster or a very senior detective was being buried. As the camera covered the Princess's progress toward the royal box, he had no difficulty picking out the other guards, thick around the box itself, then thinning out until by a hundred feet from the Princess there were only individuals on the corner of every stairway. They were easy to spot; they were all wearing large sport coats, and unlike everyone else they were not watching the Princess. One of them, a Brit, Salter guessed, from the thickness of the cloth of his jacket, was now opening the door of the royal box. The cameras swept the packed Woodbine stands while the commentators in their pink jackets chattered on about the lovely day, the beautiful Princess, and the record crowd.

Security at the track looked as if it would be a huge problem, but in fact it was less difficult than on the street. The place had been swept clean in the morning, and after that, everyone, first the employees, then the crowds, had been screened by mechanical detectors and scrutinized by the guards as they passed through the gates and turnstiles. Then, three-quarters of an hour before the big race, the track was locked up tight, and the latecomers had to wait until the Princess had come and gone, forced to make small bets among themselves. Several hotels overlooked the track in such a way as to offer a possible burrow for a sharpshooter and they, too, had been emptied of all their guests on the upper floors.

There was a shot of the track from high up showing the whole scene, followed by a shot of the Goodyear blimp which provided the overhead view. The preparations for the race had now gone on long enough, and Salter began daydreaming, wondering if anyone had ever written a thriller involving the hijacking of the Goodyear blimp, and wondering whose job it was to make sure that the blimp had not already been taken over by a gang of maniacs. Finally the race was run, and the Princess came out of her box to congratulate the used-car dealer who owned the winner, and give him fifty guineas. Salter noticed that the atmosphere around the Princess was changing. Suddenly, instead of climbing back into the Governor-General's carriage to make her exit down the track, she was slipped into one of the waiting limousines that had materialized and was driven away before the crowd was aware anything was happening. And instead of any more descriptions of her hat, a sports commentator appeared to give the details of the next race. Shortly afterwards there was an announcement that a bomb had exploded in a garage on Yorkville Avenue, within ten yards of the route that the Princess had walked that morning. A man was dead, and a panel truck destroyed.

"Jesus Christ," Salter said, grabbing his jacket and running for the door. "I'll call in," he shouted over his shoulder.

Yonge Street was clear as far as St. Clair Avenue. After that, he had to use his red dot to get past the swarm of yellow police cars and motorcycles filtering the traffic away from Yorkville. When he reached the village, Yorkville Avenue was blocked to all cars, including his, and he abandoned his car behind the library and began to run the two blocks to the garage. The closer he got the more it seemed as if the police were holding a convention in the streets; at the corner of Bay and Yorkville even his red dot had to be backed up by flashing his identity card to get any farther.

Three fire trucks blocked the approaches to the garage, effectively jamming in a number of other vehicles—ambulances, police cars, and some civilian cars whose owners were being shoved away from the area. (Afterwards, Salter heard that road blocks had been set up on every highway out of the city.) Inside the garage, there was no fire that he could see, the explosion having failed to ignite the gas tank. A solid wall of police prevented anyone from approaching that corner of the basement, and beyond them he could see a swarm of technicians and photographers. Salter found the staff superintendent in charge and showed his identification.

"What do you want?" the man said, not looking at Salter.

"My job this morning was to keep the street traders out of the area. This bomb was probably set by them. I think I spoke to the girl who rigged it. We can find her and her pals in ten minutes. My man is with them now."

"What the hell are you talking about?"

"The van that was bombed. It was theirs."

The superintendent took him by the arm and pulled him to one side, out of the little ring that was forming to listen to Salter. "I'm still not with you, pal," he said. "Who are 'they'?"

"The street traders. They owned the van."

The superintendent shook his head. "Take a look. C'm'ere." He pushed Salter through the police into the corner of the basement. In the last parking space was the wreckage of the bombed van. Although it looked a total write-off, it was clearly a plain dark blue Toyota, not a wizard's Chevrolet. The street traders' van was still in its place, twenty-five feet away.

Salter's first reaction was relief that he hadn't screwed up. The security that was supposed to prevent bomb attacks from any quarter was not his responsibility, thank God. It was probably the job of the superintendent, the man who still had him by the arm. Salter calmed down and took a closer look at the van. The front windows were blown out and the driver's door was swinging from one hinge, but the rest of the van was still in one piece.

"Whose truck is it? Stolen?"

"No, the owner put it here this morning. It belongs to a store on Cumberland. Lilliput. Some kind of bookstore."

"According to the news, there was a guy killed. I think I might have met him," Salter said. "Where is he? Did you identify him?"

"The owner's husband. Guy named Pearson. You knew him?"

Salter shook his head, feeling defeated. Two more men appeared. "Who's in charge?" one of them asked. Neither man was wearing an identity disk.

The superintendent identified himself and one of the men flashed a card. "That it?" he asked. "Go and have a look, Fred." The other man walked over to the wreck, sniffed the air, looked around the walls and ceiling, and returned to his colleague. "Nothing to do with us," he reported. The accent, Salter now heard, was British.

"How do you know?" the superintendent asked.

The two men walked away from the group. The superintendent followed them, beckoning behind him for Salter to join the group.

"It's a tiddly bit of dynamite, is my guess," the man called Fred began. "Designed to knock off the driver. It couldn't have happened in a safer place as far as we're concerned. Look at it. This place is like a bomb shelter. If it was anyone trying to upset us it would have been organized a bit different. A lot different. No, this is a bit of local bother. Something for you people to worry about."

One of the explosives squad now interrupted. "We found this," he said, showing them a small metal plate with a button set in it.

"That settles it, then," the first Englishman said. "Your problem."

"Why?" the superintendent said, irritated. "How?"

"Tell him." The Englishman gestured to the explosives expert and turned away to confer with his colleague.

"It's the trigger," the expert said to the superintendent. "Designed to activate the charge. We found it on the floor outside the truck, but it might have been under the seat or under the tire. Either it went off as soon as the driver got in, or as soon as he moved the van."

"So it wasn't meant for throwing and it wasn't meant to bother us," the Englishman said over his shoulder. "A little local bother. Seen enough, Neville?"

The other Englishman nodded and the two walked off.

Salter said, "I'm not sure if this is anything to do with me, either. I'm not in Homicide."

"Somebody must care," the superintendent said. "Me, I suppose. All right, Salter. If it's your problem you'll soon find out."

SALTER PUSHED HIS WAY through the crowd and left the garage through the Cumberland exit. He walked along the street to the Lilliput bookstore, which was locked up and dark. While he was standing on the steps, peering down, wondering who would want to kill the husband of the bookstore owner with a bomb, unable to believe it was any of the peddlers he had been watching, he became aware of someone behind him, delivering a monologue for his benefit.

"I'm getting out," the voice said. "Could be anybody next. I thought you were looking after us. I'm not stopping here."

It was Vera, delivering herself of her verdict. She was speaking almost quietly, obviously badly frightened. "I knew something was going to happen," she continued. "I knew it. Whoever it is, I'm not going to be the next one he kills."

"I told you," Salter said. "Don't panic."

"Don't panic, he says. Sit here and get killed. No fear. Not unless you get rid of all those street traders."

"You think the bomb was planted by them?"

"Of course it was them. Who do you think did it?"

"You could be wrong, you know. But someone will be around. The investigating officer. Tell him." He broke free from her as she continued her monologue. What she was saying made him realize that the quiet time was over, because if she thought the traders were behind the bomb, then others would, too. He went back to the garage and made a note of the dead man's identification, his full name and address, and caught a ride with a squad car back to his office, leaving his car where he had parked it.

III

SEVEN

THE HEADQUARTERS BUILDING was just beginning to settle down. There were far more people about than usual on a Saturday afternoon, but many of them, looking slightly unbuttoned after the panic, were getting ready to leave as it became accepted that the British were probably correct that the bombing was unconnected with the Princess. It had become an incident to be dealt with by normal procedures. But, as Salter had suspected, there was still hardly anyone available to look after ordinary police work, and Salter got the job.

"Staff Superintendent Orliff is looking for you," the switchboard informed him when he checked for messages. He took off his jacket and walked along to Orliff's office, wondering what the staff superintendent was doing in the building.

"They called me in to look after this thing," Orliff said. "Everybody else is busy. She's going to be here for four more days and this bomb's made them nervous, even if it wasn't meant for her. Even the boys you had this afternoon are needed. But you know what they say, every day that goes by decreases the chance of catching a villain by fifty percent. So I have to begin the investigation and hand it over to Homicide when they're back to normal. That is," he said, smiling, "I'd like you to begin it. I was just waiting for you to come back. Cup of coffee?" Orliff unscrewed the cap of a large thermos jug. "I figured nothing would be working around here, so I brought some in."

Typical Orliff, thought Salter, looking around the immaculate office, at the neat stacks of paper on Orliff's desk, and at Orliff himself, who looked as he always did, pen in hand, ready to open the file on the bombing, keeping a complete record of every move he made, thinking of everything, including, now, the possibility that the canteen might be closed on a Saturday afternoon. Salter accepted the coffee and sat down.

"Am I working on my own?" he asked.

"When does Gatenby get back?"

"Not for another week."

Orliff made a note and thought about the problem. "Ranovic?"

Salter nodded. "He won't be enough, though. I will want him to stay with the peddlers, just in case he hears something. I need someone else for the legwork."

"There *isn't* anybody else." Orliff tapped the sheet of paper. "Hang on." He left the office and Salter heard him going down the stairs to the front offices. He returned within a few minutes and picked up his pencil. "You can keep Ranovic," he said. "But watch him. He's got a string of reprimands, that one."

"What for?"

"Petty stuff. Not reporting in enough. Not filling out his notebook properly. Going beyond his orders."

"Does he use hard drugs?"

"Not that we know of. He's not one of those. He just won't stick to the rules. Not a very good team man."

"He did a good job today."

"Yeah, well, keep him on a short rein. He's been undercover so long he's probably forgotten where his uniform is. He needs to be reminded."

"Who else?"

"I was just looking. There's a new kid in Public Affairs that Walters says we can have. I grabbed him before someone else did. He looks pretty green. Name's Brennan, right out of police college."

"Okay. They must have taught him how to do legwork. How long do I have? Am I filling in time until Her Royal Highness goes away?"

"About a week, I'd say. When she goes, everyone will want a day off, then you can hand it over. I'm sorry about this."

Salter looked up, surprised. "Why? It doesn't seem so terrible."

"It's a bad time to give you a case you won't be able to finish."

"Why? Why is it a bad time now?"

Orliff picked up the phone. "No calls until I tell you," he said. He walked around the desk and shut the door.

Salter became concerned. Orliff was not given to dramatics. Whatever was coming was serious, and Salter ran through his actions of the past few days to see what sins he had committed, but there was nothing.

Orliff said, "I'm taking early retirement. I'm leaving this summer. I was going to tell you next week. It just came through. Somebody else will be doing this job."

Later, Salter remembered that Orliff had made a real effort to let him know as soon as possible, and he eventually became grateful. Now, though, his reaction was a selfish, low-level desire to talk Orliff out of it. "Why?" he asked. "Why now?"

"Because this is the first day I could do it, the day I've been waiting for for ten years. My pension will keep us, and I've got enough money, with a little mortgage on the house, to build that cottage. I've made it, Charlie, reached retirement with something to retire for. And with." He patted the pile of "cottage" papers on his desk.

"Who's going to take over?" Salter asked. He ran through the possibilities in his mind, flinching from several of them, one most of all. "Will they give it to Cresswell?" he asked. If so, he knew he would not last long. Superintendent Cresswell prided himself on being a hard man, who, if he had his way, would begin the day by leading his men through an hour's physical jerks in the parking lot. He was also, in Salter's opinion, very stupid.

Orliff allowed himself a sympathetic snort. "Don't worry about Cresswell," he said. "And don't speculate anymore. Wait and see."

But it was too serious to be dismissed like that. Any change would surely be for the worse. Was this it, then? What he had been preparing himself for? Time to quit?

Orliff said, "It would have been better if we had ended with a case we'd solved, like that woman who was strangled."

"You think this bombing job is going to make us look bad?"

"It's insoluble, Charlie. It took me no time to figure that out. We'll wind up with an open file."

"Why?"

"They say it was explosives, triggered by a battery. To me that means a professional. I don't know why the mob would want to take out this guy, or why anyone would, but it was done by a pro, you can bet your life. And we're never going to nail anyone with it."

"We don't know that yet. It might still be the street traders, or somebody in his personal life. Maybe the thing wasn't meant for him. You can't just say that it was a pro and go through the motions."

"Nor will we. You'll spend the next week, until we get back to normal, eliminating all the possibilities. That's what I'm saying. But that's enough of that. I just wanted to let you know what was happening to me before you heard it on the grapevine."

"Thanks. If Cresswell does take over, you think I should ask for a transfer?"

"Never mind who is going to take over. Do I think you should ask for a transfer? Where to? Homicide? You've done them a favor in the past."

Salter shook his head. "No, they're too clannish."

"Public Affairs? Community Relations? Where?"

But wherever Salter looked, the grass seemed less green. "I'll wait and see."

"That's right. Now go and find the bomber. Lotsa luck. Your street traders are in Room 411. Sergeant O'Leary brought them in. He's next door making up his report. I told him you'd take them off his hands. Keep me posted."

SALTER FOUND THE TRADERS in the disused office, being watched over by a young policewoman.

"Hey, there, Inspector," the girl he had found in the van called as he walked in. "You come to take us away from all this?"

"I'll be back in a minute." Salter went next door to the sergeant who had taken them in.

"We found them in a coffee shop on Avenue Road," the sergeant said. "Your guy, Constable Ranovic, told us where they were. I took a statement. They were on Hazelton Avenue all day, except one, the girl in the long skirt, and Ranovic says you know about her. Ranovic can vouch for the rest of them. He was there until the bomb went off and then he stayed nearby keeping an eye on them. I didn't know what I was supposed to charge them with, so I just shoved them in the room until someone took them off me. Superintendent Orliff says that's you.''

Salter nodded. ''I thought they were harmless, but bombs are bombs. Okay, I'll take it from here.''

''Can I have Lucy back now?''

''As soon as I'm finished. It won't take long.''

''Tell her I'll be here when she's through, will you?''

SALTER WENT first to look for Ranovic. He found him in the deserted cafeteria, reading a newspaper account of the Princess's arrival in Toronto. When Salter appeared, he leaped to his feet, clicked his heels, shouted ''Sir'' like an English sergeant-major, and stood rigid, waiting for his orders. It was the hint that Salter had missed before, the clue as to why Ranovic had such a spotty record. There was a touch of the clown in him which did not always surface at the most appropriate times. Subordinates, like children, are difficult to discipline if they horse around with their roles, and the parent or superior can be sure that the most genial clowning contains an edge of mockery. Salter decided to ignore Ranovic's fooling as long as he did what he was told. He sat down opposite the constable and waited for Ranovic to sit also, which he did, facing Salter, arms across his chest and back straight. But his marine-recruit impersonation was in such contrast to the thick tangle of black hair, his elegant costume, and most of all to the thin, dark nervous face now trying to look stolid that Salter was sure that Ranovic was still, slightly, sending him up, whether Ranovic knew it or not.

''I'm going to start with the street traders,'' Salter said. ''How many were there altogether in that group you were with?''

''Five, counting me.''

"We'll say four, then, shall we, on the outside chance that you're on our side? Did you get any idea of whether there was anyone else?"

"Just Rosie Porlock, in the van."

"I'll look after her. On second thought I'll look after them all. You stay under, see what you can hear. I'll investigate you, too. These four, did any of them have a license to sell in Yorkville?"

"No, none of them."

"So who have we got? Go down the list."

Ranovic pulled a sheet of paper from his wallet. "I already did. First there's Rosie—sells jewelry, makes it herself."

"Know anything about her?"

"I think she's the brains, the leader. Yesterday the others all acted sort of—waiting for the word from her, you know? None of them seemed to be in charge."

"Who are the others?"

"George Miner, sells leather belts, purses, and such. Big, soft guy; very earnest. Then there's Fiona Sander, sells sweaters she makes herself. A real knockout. Used to be a model, they say. I wouldn't doubt it. Then there's Moira Pitt, tough little broad, sells miniature paintings of Toronto scenes."

"She's an artist?"

"Nah." Ranovic shook his head, grinning. "I saw her take delivery one morning. Somebody runs a sweatshop somewhere, churning these things out. But Moira undersells the Erudite Dwarf."

"Who?"

"The Erudite Dwarf. It's a store on Yorkville that sells dollhouses mainly, but all kinds of other small stuff. He's got Shakespeare plays in books about one inch square. Miniatures, not condensed. The owner's about six feet tall, so I guess he's making some kind of joke. The place is always jammed."

"But he didn't get a threatening letter."

"No, and I don't think he minds Moira. She's only got the one item and it's just a little sideline for him."

"That it?"

"That's the lot, except for Archie, who sells balloons and those twirly things kids like."

"Why these?"

"What do you mean? Why what?"

"Are these four—five—all buddies?"

"Oh, I see. Yeah, I think they are. They're all young. Under thirty. I mean they're not like the old Italian guy who's been selling chestnuts all his life. These are trying out different lifestyles, I think. Fiona doesn't eat meat."

"Are they dropouts?"

"No, Rosie has some kind of degree. No, they work hard as hell. You have to out on the street."

"Are they making a living?"

"Oh, sure." Ranovic grinned again. "I'm doing okay. I'm thinking of setting up my kid brother. I could take twenty-five percent off the top of his sales and still put him through university. Right now he's getting minimum wage for washing windows."

"What were they up to? It was harmless enough, wasn't it?" Salter looked at his notes. "All Rosie wanted to do was wave a placard. Were the others very serious about upsetting the parade?"

"They were excited, like kids on a dare, which is what they were."

"You think if Rosie planted a bomb they would know about it?"

"Come on, boss. These people are harmless. They don't know bombs."

"Rosie?"

Ranovic shrugged. "Okay, her I don't know. She's kinda strange."

"All right. Stay out of the way until I'm through."

Salter walked to the door after Ranovic left and called to the policewoman to send in Rosie Porlock.

"Hey," she said, as she walked in. "Hey, I just carry banners, try to get the cameras on me. I don't bomb things. I don't know how."

She was not protesting. Her manner was conversational, interested. Salter saw that she probably talked like that to everybody. She was at home in the world, more curious than threatened by it, even in a police station. She looked around the room. "You should get some plants in here," she said. "It's pretty hostile." She sat down, leaning forward, her feet wide apart.

"So tell me," Salter began, "when did you park in the garage? Was the other van there already? Did you see anyone else? The whole thing you can remember."

"Trouble is, chief, I was down on the floor of the van so no one could see me. I couldn't see out." Her face registered a new thought. "Hey, I was lucky, wasn't I? They could've mistimed the thing. I might have gotten hurt. I was sitting next to a bomb for about five hours. Wow!"

"When did you park your truck? What time?"

"Five to nine. Just before they closed the gate."

"Was the other truck there?"

"I think so."

"Who was the one the police found in your van?"

"Henry. You guys were supposed to find him."

Salter looked at her quizzically.

"We figured if they found Henry, they wouldn't look for anyone else in the same van. Worked, too, didn't it?"

Salter smiled. "Clever. So did you see or hear anything?"

"How do you mean?"

"Anyone moving around the other truck? Anything like that?"

"Oh, sure. Lots. But I was crouched down, see, and I couldn't look up when anyone was around. Faces show up in the dark. I had to look *down*."

"You heard voices around the truck?"

"Voices. Sure, two or three times."

"Would you recognize them again?"

"Maybe. Which station were they from?"

"What?"

"All the voices I heard were cops. At least they were talking cop stuff. All about overtime, and whether they had to wear white gloves that night. Stuff like that. One guy was bitching about having to declare his plainclothes allowance to the income-tax people."

"And that's it?"

"That's it. Nobody said, 'Here's the bomb, Ivan. Put it under the hood.' 'Right you are, Sergei. My, that's a strange scar you've got under your left eye. Just like an arrowhead.' Sorry."

"All right. Go back and sell your junk, but tell the desk sergeant where we can find you."

George Miner was next, a large, soft-faced man with wispy fair hair on his chin which he fingered continually as if it were a real beard. Salter established very quickly that Rosie had planned the whole intervention and Miner's job was to lead the others in the protest on Hazelton Avenue.

"Why only five of you?" Salter asked.

"The others were afraid. They figured you would beat us up, and they'd lose their licenses for good."

"*You* didn't, though."

"I figured you would get too much negative publicity if you tried anything like that." Miner spoke in a slowed-down, deadened voice like a malfunctioning record player, and the effect was to fill the listener with boredom in three sentences.

"Did any of you send any threatening letters?" Salter asked, thinking, you have to ask, sometimes someone says, yes, sir, I killed him, in reply to the question, a thing he would not have volunteered but which his upbringing makes it impossible to deny if asked directly.

"You already asked us that. No, sir, I did not."

"Do you know who did?"

"No. It was no one in our group. We think it was one of the regular merchants."

"Why?"

"To make us unpopular, provoke you people into harassing us. That's how it worked."

Salter ignored this. "Apart from your little gang, did you see or hear anyone doing anything suspicious while you were in the area, getting ready to march?"

Miner stroked his chin hairs. "There was one man who was not in our group originally, but we let him join us because he said he was going to cause a disruption on his own, which might have gotten in the way of ours. I don't think he was even a regular street trader. He could be someone you should investigate."

"Is he waiting outside now?"

"No. That's another thing that's suspicious. How did he get missed when you were picking us up?"

"What's he like? What's he sell?"

"He calls himself Bruno."

"Thanks." Salter made a show of noting down the name. Was there a smile buried in those soft, hairy cheeks? Did Miner know that Ranovic was a cop?

The other two were no more rewarding than Miner. They were a group who had in common that they had gone into street trading as an alternative to the lives they might have led. They all came from fairly conventional backgrounds, and it was this that made them protest, knowing their rights, while most of the other street traders knew that their rights were what the police felt like allowing them and conducted themselves accordingly. When the police said move, they moved, and moved back when the cops themselves moved on.

After Salter was finished with them, Ranovic came out of the room where he had been keeping out of sight.

"A small problem," Salter said. "I think they're on to you."

"You mean my cover's blown?"

"Right. But we're going to try to lift you out. Be in Queen's Park tonight at midnight. When you hear the helicopter, give him the signal. One long flash, two short ones. He'll make just one pass. It's your only chance."

But Ranovic the clown could not detect irony when it was directed at his image of himself. "Huh?" he asked.

Salter didn't bother to explicate the joke. "Miner knows you're not a street trader," he said.

Ranovic, still working on Salter's fantasy, shook his head. "He doesn't know I'm a cop. There's no way. What did he say?"

Salter repeated the conversation with Miner. Ranovic pounced on it. "Don't you see? He just wants you to look somewhere else. I'm not one of his crowd, is all he means, so he's letting you have me so you'll leave them alone. Listen, tomorrow I'll go out there. I'll be pretty hostile, see, because you've given me a rough time and I figure they've been pointing a finger at me, just like Miner did. But they'll think I'm clean; otherwise you'd never have let me back on the street. They'll be sorry, see, and I could get real close to them.''

Salter looked skeptical. ''Or they could figure out the obvious, that you're a cop.''

''No way.'' Ranovic shook his head vehemently. ''I've been working undercover for the drug squad for six months and if I can fool the bikers, you think I can't fool a bunch of peddlers, for God's sake! No, let me stay out there. If there's anything to hear, I'll hear it.''

Salter remained unconvinced. ''These people, Rosie Porlock and Miner especially, don't strike me as stupid.''

''They're babes in the woods. I can handle them.''

''Okay, go back there and open up for business as usual. But don't screw around. If you aren't doing any good there I need you to help with the checking. So if you get a hint that they do know who you are—if you've blown your cover, like—I want to know right away. I'll let this gang go now. Stay here for a minute.'' Salter left the office, closing the door behind him, and told the policewoman that the traders could go.

''On the other hand, boss,'' Ranovic said, when Salter had resumed his seat. ''I may be wasting my time, anyway. As I said, these people are babes in the woods. There's no way they could plant bombs.''

''Probably. But if you make certain of that, then you won't be wasting my time, which is what matters.''

Ranovic jerked himself rigid and gave a mock American air force salute. ''Yessir,'' he said.

''I'm going to try to talk to the man's wife tomorrow morning, and afterwards take a look at his apartment.'' He checked a note on his desk. "It's on Bloor Street. Meet me there at noon." He gave Ranovic the address.

All this was routine, and Salter went through it with half his mind, while the other half stayed on Orliff's resignation, and on his own future.

Finally he talked to Constable Brennan, a recruit whose near baldness only emphasized his shining newness, like a new-laid egg, and whose eagerness to be of service made him hard to look at directly. Salter told him that Ranovic would fill him in on the area he was covering, and told him what he wanted to know. "It's routine," Salter said. "Start with the garage, then question every storekeeper in the immediate vicinity who was around today. Find out what they noticed, what caught their eye after the Princess went by. Did they see anyone they recognized go into the garage? It's a tedious job and you won't get anywhere, but once in a million years you do find out something, and anyway it's got to be done."

"What's the name of the officer who's briefing me?" Brennan asked, already preparing to make his first entry in his notebook.

"Huh?" Salter asked. "Oh, right. Ranovic. Constable Ranovic. He's waiting in the next office. He's wearing white pants and a kind of black sweatshirt."

"Plainclothes?"

What makes you think that? That's his uniform. He's in the marine division. "Yes, that's what I was trying to say. Plainclothes."

Brennan went off smartly to look for Ranovic while Salter entertained himself wondering what language the two constables would use to talk to each other, street talk or officialese. It kept his mind off Orliff for a few minutes.

It was seven o'clock. Salter considered his next move. If Orliff was right and the bomb had been planted by a professional, there wasn't much to be gained by rushing around looking for a relative or a friend who had a grudge against the dead man, and all the possibilities that lay behind the hiring of a professional could wait until tomorrow. Yorkville would still be jammed, the regular Saturday night crowd swollen by sightseers come to stare at the garage. He gave the switchboard a brief statement for the press that the bombing was an "isolated incident unconnected with the royal visit," told the operator to pass the statement on to the duty inspector, and went home.

AFTER DINNER, Annie said, "Don't sweat about them. Let them alone."

"Who? Seth and Dad?"

"No. Angus and Angie. Isn't that what you're brooding about?"

"No." And then he told her what was on his mind.

Annie listened in silence, then hunched herself like someone with a lot to say. Salter recognized the signals. "What do you think I should do?" he asked her.

She shrugged and shook her head, staying silent and hunched.

"No advice?"

She allowed some more time to elapse. Then, "How long will it take?"

"What?"

"Before you know."

"Could be a week, could be a month. Why?"

"I just want to be prepared."

"For what?"

"Coping with you." Then it came in a steady flow. "We went through this four years ago when Tempest retired, and you thought you were washed up. It was a very bad time around here.''

"Was I that bad?"

"You were impossible. For months. Every day. It was like treading on eggs. Even the kids stayed away from you. At the time I thought it was part of being married, one of the stages. I even wondered if it was me, if you wanted to stay married. I was hoping you'd quit the force.''

"I remember. But I told you, I'm a policeman.''

"I remember, too. I remember wondering how long it was going to go on. And then it got all right again. You got some good assignments and this Special Affairs Center came along and it seemed perfect.''

Salter smiled. "Too good to last." He looked across at Annie, who was staring at the blank television screen. "Maybe I will quit," he said with an interrogative note in his voice. "You wanted me to then.''

"It's not the same. Then I was saying, do it if you must, I'm with you all the way. Whither thou goest, I go. You know? Now I don't have to stand behind you, or by your side, or whatever. You see what I mean?''

"No."

"I've got a job, Charlie, like you. I'm doing well. Whatever you decide it may not change my life very much, so it's really your decision.'' For three years Annie had worked her way steadily up the advertising ladder and now worked for a production house, making commercials. Pleased for her, Salter had not yet begun to think of her career as more than a hobby. Now she was telling him.

"You mean you don't care, one way or the other. Okay.''

She ignored the provocation this offered. "What I care about is that you understand that you should not worry about me or the boys or this lot.'' She waved her hand around the room. "We're all right now. Your pension, my job, the money from my grandmother—it adds up to the fact that you can do what you like. If you stay in a situation you don't like, that's your decision, not your duty."

"So I should quit."

"Not necessarily, for God's sake! Or if you do, quit while you're ahead. Don't wait until you're down again. You've had a good spell. Take the money and run."

"And do what?"

"I don't know. Consult one of these professional agencies. Open a marina. I don't know. But let's try and keep the good thing going."

There was a silence for several minutes before Annie began again.

"What, exactly, did Orliff say?"

Salter recounted the conversation as accurately as he could.

Annie said, "It sounds to me as if he knows who is going to take over."

"Why?"

"He told you not to worry about Cresswell. That's a pretty strong statement from Orliff, isn't it?"

"But later on, when I asked him if I should transfer, he suggested some possibilities."

"That's because you hadn't been listening to him. Why did he tell you he was retiring in the first place?"

"So that I wouldn't hear it on the grapevine, he said."

"So he's thinking about you. He said don't do anything stupid. Don't do anything. He knows, all right, and he's told you to sit still. So take his advice. Wait and see. Find the mad bomber."

"He said it was a bad time for me to get a case I couldn't solve."

"Why? He's up to something, Charlie. He trying to sell you to your next boss. Something like that. But being Orliff, he doesn't talk about it. Sit tight, and if it doesn't work out, walk away from it then. You're past the point where it matters, except on a day-to-day basis."

"You mean I'm too old?"

"Not to enjoy the job. And to quit if you don't. No, but you're—what's the word—controversial. Too controversial to make deputy chief. That's why I like you. Do whatever you like, but remember that we're all right if you are, only we don't want to live with you for the next five years watching you hate your job."

EIGHT

RUTH PEARSON had been saved the grisly job of identifying her husband by Leese, her friend. When Salter called on Sunday morning to tell her he was coming, she was clear-voiced and apparently calm. Salter found her at home on Dupont Street, a few houses in from Avenue Road, within easy walking distance of her store. The house looked well-kept, still true to its origins with no signs of having been face-lifted. Leese met Salter at the door and took him around to the back, where another pleasant surprise awaited him. Instead of a deck or a patio, there was a yard, a comfortable grassy space made shady by a giant Manitoba maple. Ruth Pearson was sitting in a Cape Cod chair, another chair empty by her side, waiting for him.

"I'll be upstairs if you want anything," Leese said.

"Don't go far away, Mr. Leese. I'd like to talk to you later," Salter said. Leese looked slightly surprised in a way that Salter felt he was intended to notice, nodded, and left.

Salter sat down and loosened his tie. June had struck Toronto with a blast of humidity, and Salter's clothes felt like three layers of blankets. The Princess had been reported as looking faint during yesterday's festival. Today she was resting before sallying forth to open an old folks' home in Mississauga.

Leese reappeared with a glass full of ice cubes and clear liquid. "Tonic without gin," he said. "Want some?"

"Sure," Salter said, reaching for it.

"Is there enough ice, David? I defrosted the fridge yesterday, and it may not have made enough."

Don't worry about it, thought Salter. Just tell your cocktail guests your husband was blown up yesterday. They'll understand. He removed his jacket. "This may take a few minutes," he said.

She nodded. "We've been talking about it, David and I. When a bomb goes off in my van and kills my estranged husband there are a lot of possibilities, aren't there? Was it meant for me? By whom? Was it meant for him? Again, by whom? Or was it just a bomb, someone trying to make everyone nervous with the Princess around? Any others?"

"The wrong van, maybe?"

"Whose van could they have mistaken it for?"

"One of the street traders had a van in there, near yours."

"You mean someone wanted to blow up one of the street traders? Those harmless little people? Dear God. That one didn't occur to us."

"It's just one possibility, without considering the people involved. Not very likely."

"Good. Let's get started, then." She crossed her legs and looked at him expectantly. "Is your drink all right?" She faced Salter with the air of someone determined to be sensible in a crisis. Only the way she carefully attended to all the details of ordinary life betrayed the effort she was making to behave normally.

"Let's start with the van. It belongs to the business? The store?"

"That's right. It's registered as the bookstore's van, but I don't have another car. I used it for everything."

"Did your husband have a car?"

"Surely, but . . . we didn't cohabit, Inspector. We were getting ready to be divorced. I'm marrying David Leese, the man you have met."

"How long have you been separated?"

"A year, more or less, but my husband moved out for good after Christmas. For a year before that we had the same address, but I already had David."

"Did your husband have a friend? A woman friend?"

"Not that I know of."

"For two years?" Salter's real question hung in the air.

"As far as I know. It was one of the points he was making in the divorce, that it was I who wanted it, not him. In the old days we would have been in court talking about adultery, mine, and he was trying to get all the mileage he could out of it. In other words he was contesting the divorce."

"Why?"

"Money." She lifted her glass but put it back on the table without drinking. "The only good thing is that we have no children to fight over. We're fighting over everything else. Were. The house, the shop, everything."

"It was all jointly owned?"

"Yes, and he could claim that both the house and the store were bought or begun on his income. It's true, technically, but it isn't really true. He made the down payment on this house, and then he agreed to let me take out a second mortgage to start the store. When the store did well enough, some of the profits went into repairing the house. And then there's my labor, as a housewife and in the store. I was going to win if it came down to the wire, but he was going to make it a very messy business."

"Why? Why was he so hostile?"

"He wasn't really. That was his bargaining position. We wouldn't have gone all the way. I would have bought him off, which was what he was really after."

"Did he need the money?"

"Yes, he did. He was just about to start a new business himself, some sort of store."

"Did he have a job?"

"Not a proper job. He got cut back in the last recession and hadn't been able to find anything in his line since. Can I get you another drink?"

"No, thanks. What did he do?"

"He was a copywriter, advertising, but he couldn't find anyone to hire him, because they thought he was used up, I think. Anyway, he had trouble finding a job, so he started his own business. Name generation."

"What happens now?" Salter wrote "name generation" in his notebook.

"That's what I'm wondering. A long time ago we took out policies on each other as partners in the store, and I've kept the premiums up, so now I'll collect, I guess, as soon as you find out who did it. And if he hasn't changed his will in the meantime, without telling me. I'm his heir for anything else he's got. It won't be much. What I'll really get is the store and the house, which suits me fine. Suddenly I'm all right again. I've got a house, a store, and a lover I want to marry." She put her feet together and smoothed her hair. "The obvious person to plant a bomb was me, but I didn't." She looked at Salter suddenly and determinedly.

"What is 'name generation'?" Salter asked.

"He made up names. When a company invents a new product, or changes an old one, or when it wants to change its own name, then the name generators think one up. It's become a profession. But there again, I don't think my husband was very good at it, hence the latest idea, to get out of the whole advertising game and start his own store."

Leese appeared. "Now, I'm making coffee," he said. "Anyone else?"

Salter shook his head. Ruth Pearson waggled her nearly full glass and smiled at Leese. "No, thanks, darling. But we ought to think about food, shouldn't we? Arlequin is open on Sundays."

"I'll pick something up. Let's stay home." Leese disappeared.

After a long pause, she said, "I'm going to marry David but he's got a problem with a wife who is hoping for a reconciliation, so she won't talk about divorce yet. But he lives here. She thinks I have seduced him and made him temporarily insane. He does have children. They are trying to help their parents to work it out."

Salter was silent. Nothing about the lives of people who lived south of St. Clair Avenue surprised him.

He returned to a question in his notebook. "What was your husband doing in the store's van?" he asked.

"He was borrowing it. Don't forget he owned half of it. Periodically he would simply demand the van for a weekend, just to show he had the right to, I think. I always let him have it. This time he wanted it for something to do with his own store."

"What kind of store was it to be?"

"You know L. L. Bean?"

"The one in Maine?"

She nodded. "He figured that Canada was ready for its own L. L. Bean. A lot of Canadians go on annual pilgrimages to Freeport in Maine to buy things we can't get here, or that cost twice the price in Toronto. He thought the demand was there so he took a lease on a place on Bayview Avenue and he was going to open up next month. He wanted the truck to move some stuff."

"What kind of stuff?"

"A typewriter; a special chair for his back; some files. He had been using his apartment as an office; now he was going to work at his new store—he was still doing a bit of name generating—so he wanted to move his things over."

"When did he get the keys of the van from you?"

She shook her head. "He didn't. He had his own set of keys for everything, for the van, and for this house, too, though he never came here unannounced once he'd moved out. I could have had all the locks changed but I was walking a tightrope and I didn't want to do anything he could use against me later. Besides, he had a vicious temper." She made the remark in a judicious way, without obvious passion.

"So you parked the van in the garage on Saturday morning for him to pick up. When was he supposed to return it?"

"Monday. But he might have kept it longer just to show he had the right to. He did that occasionally."

"Did anyone else know he was borrowing the van that weekend?"

"David, of course. But it wasn't a secret. I can't think of anyone else I told specifically, but anyone might have overheard me talking about it."

Salter sipped the rest of his tonic water and consulted his notebook. He made an ostentatious tick on one page, then put the book away. "You have any enemies that you know of?" he asked.

"Not now. Is that a gross thing to say?"

Salter shrugged, and she continued. "What else should I do now? It's a bit scary when this kind of thing comes close to you, when you have no idea who did it or why."

"You haven't crossed anyone in the area?"

"You mean the street traders?" She stared at him, shaking her head in disbelief. "No way, I told you, those people are harmless. I don't care what they sell, they know that. I like to see them around."

"So what did you think before I got here this morning? Why did someone bomb your van?"

"I don't know. I think it's a mistake of some kind, but I don't know who they mistook. Maybe it was just the easiest place to put a bomb that was intended for the Princess. Could that be?"

"We don't think so." Salter stood up. "Do you mind if I save myself some trouble? I have to talk to David Leese. By himself."

She jumped up. "I'll tell him. You can talk to him while I think about what we are going to eat today." She disappeared into the house and Leese emerged, looking wary and formal. He waited until Salter gave a signal, then folded himself into the chair Ruth Pearson had vacated. Salter waited for him to say something, wanting to gauge the man's emotional state, but Leese just returned his gaze. It was Salter's interview, his attitude indicated. What would he like to know?

"Somebody planted a bomb in Mrs. Pearson's van," Salter said. "At the moment I'm assuming it was meant for her." He ended on a tiny note of query. In fact, Salter was assuming nothing of the kind. He just wanted to hear Leese speak.

"That's exactly what I thought," Leese said, and shut up again.

Salter opened his notebook. "David Leese? Right? What's your address, Mr. Leese?"

"I live here."

"Officially?"

"Well, no." Leese gave an address on Duggan Avenue. "That's my wife's address, but as you've probably found out by now, I'm leaving her."

"For Mrs. Pearson."

"Yes."

"What do you do for a living?"

"I teach French."

"Which school?"

"York University."

"Ah, a professor."

"Associate."

"I'll just call you professor, shall I? Did you know the dead man?"

"The nomenclator? Of course. I was..." —here Leese paused for several seconds—"...cuckolding him."

"You were what?"

"Cuckolding him. It means..."

"I know what it means. It's a funny thing to brag about, is all." I'll look the other one up later, Salter thought.

"I'm not bragging. I thought that was the kind of thing you wanted to know. If I am sleeping with Ruth, then I have a motive for killing him, don't I?"

"I told you. It looks to me as if someone might have been trying to kill Mrs. Pearson."

"Oh, but that was just flim-flam on your part to get me to relax, I think. I just agreed with you to get *you* to relax."

Now, under cover of looking bewildered, Salter took a good look at Leese. A handsome man, elegantly got up, but under the silver hair, inside the white suit, behind the baggy face and the remarkable teeth for a man of his age (about fifty, Salter now guessed), there was, he perceived, a very nervous man trying to dispose of his nervousness with a jaunty cheekiness more appropriate for a cocktail party than a murder inquiry. "All right," he said. "Why did you do it?"

"Hmmm?"

"Why did you do it, and how?"

"Easy enough, Inspector. Half a pound of plastique taped to the battery, waiting for the current to be switched on. As to why, I think that's obvious, don't you? It was my chance to avenge myself on this beast who had made life such a living hell for the woman I loved. A man whose every whim had been orchestrated into a symphony of sadism to wring his filthy pleasure from the sacred person of my adored." Leese spoke most of the last sentence with his eyes closed, opening them at the end to show he was finished. He smiled.

Salter looked at the house, then at Leese. Then he said, "What's the matter with you? This isn't a game or a play, buddy. A man's dead. You want to answer my questions?"

Leese gave out a "*pah*" of laughter, as forced and affected as his language. "I rather thought I was, Inspector. Not your questions, but supplying you with the answers, the reasons why. Isn't that what you want?" Then, as Salter continued to look at him, Leese held up his hand. "Right," he said. "Sorry. No more. The manners of the faculty club do not belong in a murder investigation. You're quite right. Please go ahead."

Salter looked at his notes. "You knew that Pearson was to use the van. Right?"

"Yes, I did. I never saw him. He didn't come into the store yesterday afternoon."

"Why not? To avoid meeting you?"

"Oh, no, no. He had no interest in meeting me or avoiding me. He saw me as someone who was going to take care of an old wife, not as the seducer of his current one. Pearson was interested in me only for what he could squeeze out of Ruth, by playing the injured husband in court."

"Did you work in the store all day Saturday?"

"Yes, I did. I got there about eleven-thirty to relieve Ruth for lunch, and I stayed until five; that is, until we heard the news."

"Where did you go for lunch?"

"Nowhere. There was coffee and cookies in the store and I had had a late breakfast."

"You never left the store?"

"Just to have a peek at the Princess. With Ruth."

The game was winding down now. Leese no longer seemed nervous, but Salter was beginning to realize that Leese was never unself-conscious, that he was incapable of not overhearing himself and was always on the lookout for role-playing in himself as well as in others.

Salter put his notebook away. "Who set it up, Mr. Leese?" he asked. "And why?"

Leese responded by acting as if the two of them had been chatting informally all along. "Hard to say, really," he said. "I think someone got the wrong van."

"What?"

"I think they were after the street traders. Someone put a bomb in what he thought was the street traders' van. To kill one of them." Leese appeared quite serious.

"Who? Who would go after a street trader with a bomb?"

"Another street trader?"

"Mrs. Pearson doesn't think so. She thinks they're harmless."

"Vera," a voice behind them said. "Vera hates street traders."

Salter looked around. It was Tommy Nystrom, arrived to join the postmortem.

"Enough to kill them?" Leese asked. "I think you're exaggerating, Tommy."

"I'm joking," Nystrom said. "But she does hate them."

Salter got to his feet just as Ruth Pearson reappeared with a purse in her hand. "Mr. Nystrom," he said, "I'd like to talk to you, too. Not now. Do you have an office?"

"Sort of. Over an art gallery on Berryman. If you call my machine, I'll try and meet you wherever you say." He gave Salter his card.

"Is that it, Inspector?" Ruth Pearson asked.

"For the moment. But I'll be back."

SALTER MADE HIS WAY south on Avenue Road to Bloor Street and from there he drove west until he found Pearson's address.

The door from the street opened into a small hallway. Immediately to the left, another door opened onto a corner grocery. The stairway to the apartment above began a few feet past the store entrance. Salter found Ranovic waiting in the grocery store, leafing through the magazines in the "adult" rack. They climbed the stairs to Pearson's apartment and let themselves in with the key the explosives squad had found in the bombed van.

The living room, which overlooked the street, contained a wooden couch with a padded seat and back, constructed so that it could convert into a bed by withdrawing two pegs that held the back in place. There were two canvas sling chairs, a cheap rag rug, and a square coffee table of unfinished pine. Against one wall was a green filing cabinet with a portable typewriter stored on top. The windows had roller blinds, but no other curtains. The only unfunctional thing in the room was a pile of several dozen magazines on the floor beside the couch.

The bedroom was completely empty except for a big closet which was full of good-looking clothes, including stacks of shirts and ties and underwear piled up on the built-in shelves. A heap of dirty linen was collected on the floor of the closet. The kitchen, too, was bare of furniture, but at one end was a built-in breakfast nook complete with two benches. The cupboards contained the kind and quality of dishes and cutlery that are supplied by motels which advertise kitchen facilities—a couple of saucepans, a frying pan, a teapot and an assortment of mismatched dishes and cutlery. The refrigerator contained some eggs, a loaf of bread, a carton of milk, and a bottle of club soda. There were two lasagna dinners in the freezer compartment, and the garbage container yielded the boxes from several pizzas and the wrappings of a Swiss Chalet chicken dinner. Only the bathroom seemed seriously occupied: Around the ledges were a dozen bottles and jars of hair and body-care products, and an elaborate collection of brushes and tools for tooth maintenance. The cabinet held a professional-looking collection of clippers and scissors of various kinds, straight and curved, with pointed and rounded ends.

Salter went back to the living room, where Ranovic was standing reading *Playboy*. "What do you make of this lot?" he asked, before Ranovic could ask him.

Ranovic threw himself into one of the chairs and struck a pose like Rodin's *Thinker*. "A white, Anglo-Saxon male, early middle age, who spent a lot of his time in front of a mirror. Entertained very little, and occupied himself when alone..."

Here Ranovic broke off and looked around. "Jesus, the guy didn't even have a television set. He didn't even have a *radio*."

"This is what it's like when your marriage breaks up."

"Yeah? That's it?"

"It was just a place to sleep. And take messages."

"I guess. You couldn't bring anyone here, could you?"

"It looks to me like he picked up some take-out food on his way home every night."

"And a magazine."

"Right. Came home. Ate his chicken dinner, read his magazine, and went to bed."

"What a life. I've seen jail cells that were homier than this."

"It won't take long, anyway. Check through the stuff in the bedroom closet, all the pockets, see if you can find anything at all. I'll check around here and the kitchen."

Ranovic left him and he began with the filing cabinet. It was a two-drawer affair, one drawer full of books, none of the slightest interest to Salter—inspirational biographies and financial advice—obviously thrown in the drawer when Pearson moved. The top drawer held two folders of papers. One of these contained domestic and personal papers, insurance policies, income tax receipts, and a few photographs. The other file was full of correspondence to do with Pearson's name-generating business, plus a copy of the lease on the store he was renting on Bayview Avenue. In a cupboard under the kitchen sink he found a bottle of vodka, two small cans of Bloody Mary mix, and a bottle of tonic water.

And that was all. Ranovic found nothing in the pockets of any of the clothes. "You know how to work one of those?" Salter asked, pointing to the answering machine which was attached to the telephone.

"Sure," Ranovic said. "You want me to play it back?"

Salter nodded and Ranovic ran the tape back, listening for the chatter of recorded conversation, but the tape was entirely clear. He pressed the Eject button and turned the tape over with the same result. "Either nobody ever called him, or he wiped the tape after every call," Ranovic said. Salter shrugged and picked up the two files of papers. He

made a mental note to find out where Pearson had gotten
the money to open up a store on Bayview Avenue. The
man had obviously kept his living expenses to a minimum, but what did it cost to open up a clone of L. L.
Bean?

"Let's go and have a sandwich," Salter said.

They found a restaurant on Bloor Street where Salter
ordered a hamburger and Ranovic a bowl of stir-fried
vegetables.

"That guy's apartment," Ranovic said suddenly as the
food arrived. "Real grungy, wasn't it?" He spoke with a
rising inflection, the emphasis on the "it" in the new rhetorical way.

"He lived alone. He was just camping there."

"I live alone but my place is *nice*. I've got a stereo on
one wall, and pictures. I cook stuff, too. I couldn't live like
that."

"Doesn't your girlfriend cook for you?"

"She cooks for *us*, not me. Like I do. We pretty much
share it."

"Does she live with you?"

"Not yet. We're thinking about it." Ranovic set his bowl
aside and leaned over the table. "You think I should get
married?"

Salter reared back. "How the hell do I know? If that's
what you want."

"Why did you get married?"

Salter thought of a short, brutal answer which might
embarrass Ranovic. He tried the truth. "That's what you
did, then. You met someone and got married." On Prince
Edward Island, anyway.

"It's okay, is it? You like it a lot?"

"Yes, it's okay. Yes, I like it a lot. You might not,
though." Talking to Ranovic made Salter feel as if he was

explaining his world to a Russian, say, who was thinking of defecting.

"Two kids," Ranovic went on. "I don't know. I don't know if I can relate to kids."

"What does your girlfriend think?"

"Lisa? We don't talk about it. But I wouldn't marry her. I'd have to look for someone who's more into marriage. Another thing." Ranovic looked slightly embarrassed. "Married guys I know. They screw around a lot. I don't like that. I like to have a real relationship. I don't think you ought to screw around if you have a relationship, do you?"

Salter felt unqualified to comment. "I don't know," he said. "It works for me, is all I know. Being married, I mean. Now I'm going home."

NINE

"THE BRITS ARE RIGHT," Orliff said. "No serious terrorist is going to upset anyone with a bit of dynamite in a basement garage. Maybe the 'Free Herzegovina' movement."

"What's that? A rock group?"

"Didn't you ever collect stamps? Or did it disappear before your time? Anyway, it was a personal bomb. So what are the possibilities?" He began to list them on a piece of paper. "One: Someone set out to kill Pearson. Who?"

"His wife, his wife's boyfriend, and some other boyfriend who hangs around."

"Why them?"

"Because they knew Pearson was going to use the van that day and no one else did."

"Is any one of them likely?"

"None of them is. On the face of it, that is. But I'm checking on them."

"Who else?"

"That's it. If Pearson was the intended victim it had to be someone who knew he would be using the van. Try something else."

"Someone was trying to kill Mrs. Pearson?"

"Who?"

"The peddlers."

"You think so?"

"No."

"Who else?"

"Pearson. It was an accident, maybe. He was intending to rig a bomb and it went off in his hands."

"Why should Pearson want to kill his wife?"

"He was her beneficiary. He needed money, just for living, and he was planning to open a store. Her insurance would have been very useful."

"But he was inside the van when he was killed, right? The button wouldn't be hair-trigger. He wouldn't put it under the seat while he was sitting on it, and he wouldn't get back in the van after he put it under the wheel. In either case he would be outside the van."

"If the bomb was defective?"

"If the bomb was defective, you'll never know, will you? Where would he get a bomb?"

"According to the organized crime boys, it isn't hard to buy explosives from one of the gangs. The bikers."

"Not if you're known, maybe, but that makes it less likely that Mrs. Pearson or her boyfriends are responsible. Check them out, but Pearson himself looks like the best bet."

Salter said, "Try this. What if Pearson had arranged to have his wife killed—not an unheard-of thing in this province—and got unlucky. I mean supposing they just decided to bomb the van the day he was using it."

Orliff smiled. "That would be very ironic, wouldn't it? But you'll never know that, either. That's what I said to you in the first place. A bomb looks like a pro—and maybe only Pearson could tell you. You aren't going to solve it and I'm sorry about it." He nodded to dismiss Salter.

Salter lingered after standing up. "Do you have a date yet?"

Orliff looked up. "I'll let you know as soon as I have one. By the end of the week, I would think. Are you going to ask for a transfer?"

"Not until I have to."

Orliff nodded again. "Good. I've heard nothing about who is taking over, either. I'll tell you that, too, as soon as I hear."

"Thanks." Salter would have liked to stay and talk about the future but Orliff wasn't changing his stripes in his last days. He looked after the men who worked with him but he did not share his understanding of the force's politics with any of them.

It was time to check up on Pearson, and to begin with, Salter had a number to call. That morning, before he arrived, a woman had telephoned asking for the officer in charge of the investigation into the bombing. Salter dialed the number she had left and a small, mannered female voice answered. It sounded like a woman imitating a young girl. "Hello?" the voice said. "What can I do for you?"

"Inspector Salter here. You called."

"Yes, I did. May I come and see you? It is about Mr. Pearson." The absence of the elision of the "it is" and the precision of the rest of the phrasing increased the note of artifice.

"You knew him?"

"What do you think I called for? When can I come to see you?"

"How long will it take you to get here?" Salter told her where his office was.

"I can get a cab and be there in twenty minutes."

"Now?"

"Whenever you say 'begin.' "

What is this? Salter wondered. "Come down now. I'll wait for you." He filled in his time until her arrival by calling Ruth Pearson's friend Tommy Nystrom, and made an appointment to talk to him later that morning at the bookstore.

When the woman arrived in the outer office, asking for him, Salter recognized her voice immediately; it had enormous carrying power, like a fingernail on a slate, and Salter was able to watch her progress across the outer office to the corridor outside his door before she realized that the man watching her was her objective. She walked as she talked, with neat steps, toes in line, prissy, but with a sureness of direction and purpose. The day was warm and she was dressed for it in a blue-and-white striped dress and blue sandals with high heels.

Salter got up as she reached the doorway and pointed to a chair in front of the desk. She closed the door behind her as she came in, sat down, and began immediately. "The reason I'm here, Inspector—do I call you that?—is that I do not want you coming to my house to inquire about Danny Pearson."

"Why would I do that?"

"Because somewhere in Danny's apartment there is probably a reference to me, on that machine maybe, and you would figure out all about me."

"What would I figure out? Who are you?"

The answer was obvious enough, but Salter was curious to see how she would describe herself. She was a small woman, in her early thirties, he guessed. Her body measurements looked perfect. From her ankles up through her calves, her thighs, her precisely jutting bottom, in and out for the waist, past the perfectly rounded breasts to the smooth stock of her neck, the line went without a blemish. Her carriage, too, was admirable, but her perfect and perfectly balanced figure lacked, to Salter, the necessary flaw, the too-thick ankle, the slightly plump belly that would have relieved the boredom of her neatness and charged the body with life.

Now that her voice was quieter, though, it avoided the grating edge that had come through on the phone. "The simplest thing to call me would be Danny's girlfriend. We might have gotten married. Now I would just as soon no one knew about me except that you have to. So I came here to make sure you didn't come to my house."

"Why?"

"Because I'm married, of course." Her voice, rising, once more set his teeth on edge. She took her eyes off Salter and looked briefly at the desk in front of her, like someone resting. When she resumed, her voice was very quiet. "My husband knows nothing about Danny, and I don't want him to."

"You mean you and Pearson were lovers, planning to get married, but you hadn't left your husband or told him about it. And he has no idea?"

"That's right."

"You're sure?"

"Of course I'm sure." Again the nail grated on the slate.

"If you were planning to marry Pearson you must have seen a lot of him. When did you first meet?"

"Is this important?"

Maybe, Salter thought. Interesting, anyway. "You say your husband didn't know," he said. "But let's say he did. That you made some slip. What would he have done about it?"

"I see. Good grief, you think *he* might have killed Danny? Oh, no." She shook her head several times, smiling slightly at the idea.

As much as anything, it was her underdeveloped vocabulary that lent her denial its ring of truth; her choice of idiom was both too youthful and too out-of-date, and it made her sound naïve. But the story being glimpsed seemed anything but naïve.

"Tell me why," Salter said.

"How much time do you have?"

Salter leaned back from his desk. "All you need."

"Well, to start with, I never met with Danny unless Byron was out of town."

"Byron?"

"My husband. Byron Crouch. My name is Madeline."

"What does your husband do?"

"He's a surveyor, an engineer, I guess you would call him, for an oil company. He goes out with geologists and people like that to look at new properties. He's away for weeks sometimes."

"Doesn't he have any friends?"

"Huh? Oh, who might have seen me with Danny, you mean? Oh, he had lots of buddies, but when I went out with Danny we went way out of town and he never came to the house."

"Then how else did you get together?"

"I went to his place. Nobody saw me, or if they did, no one knew who I was. Anyway, what are we talking about? Byron killing Danny, right? It's a dumb idea. Byron's up in Quebec or Labrador or someplace right now, and he's been there for weeks, so you can forget about him. Anyway, Byron's too nice, too dumb for stuff like that."

"But you were planning to leave him? How long have you been married?"

"Three years. We got married as soon as he graduated from Waterloo. Look, I married Byron to get me out of Rouyn, where we both grew up." She watched him make a note. "It's spelled R-O-U-Y-N, nearly the same as in *Madame Bovary*. It doesn't rain in Rouyn, though—it snows. And I'm no Emma, either." She waited for Salter to ask her what she was talking about. When he said nothing (he was planning to take this up at home with

Annie), she continued. "I don't think I knew then that I was marrying him just to get off the Canadian Shield, but I do now. Even before I met Danny, I realized I wasn't going to be able to live with Byron much longer, but I didn't want anything messy. Once Danny had his divorce, then I was going to handle Byron. I could have managed it without hurting him too much. He would have survived."

"Didn't Pearson mind it being secret?"

"No, why should he? It suited him perfectly. He wanted us to keep it dark until his divorce came through in case he and his wife got into a fight. Danny was the injured party, you see, so a judge would be more sympathetic. But for us the real reason was Byron."

"What happens now?"

"With me and Byron? Nothing yet. Oh, I'll leave him eventually, but in my own time. I'll wait a little while now."

"Where did you meet Pearson?"

"Through work. I'm a steno at an advertising agency. I met him at a party to celebrate some new advertising campaign."

"Then how is the affair secret? Somebody must have noticed."

"Oh, no. He made a pass at me and I turned it down. That happens all the time at work. But I don't do stuff like that. It's not fair to Byron. But when Danny persisted, said he was serious, that was different. So we worked it out that I should go over to his place and that was how it started."

"But you were going to marry him, and work on this store with him?"

"I guess so."

Salter looked at her, startled. "You *guess* so?"

"Oh, lordy, this sounds terrible, I know, but the fact is that Danny had got a bit tarnished. When I met him he seemed everything I ever wanted, but I'd gone off him a bit, now that I'd spent a lot of time with him. There wasn't as much there as I'd thought."

The kind of questions that were intriguing Salter he couldn't ask, questions that would uncover the precise degrees of emotional, sexual, intellectual, and other varieties of ties that had once bonded Pearson and this extraordinary woman together. He could not leave the subject, however, without some attempt to fill in the blanks.

"This is probably difficult for you, Mrs. Crouch, but can you give me an idea of what kind of man Pearson was? You don't have to try to be fair or objective about it. How did you see him?"

The woman, sitting straight-backed in her chair, crossed her legs, looked at her nails then at Salter. "This is a bit hard to answer, okay? I thought I was in love with Danny as recently as a month ago, but when I heard the news of his death I was a teensy bit relieved as well as shocked because lately I've been having doubts. When I first met him and for a long time he seemed like everything I needed. This name generation thing sounded like a magical way to make money, and I thought the store was another terrific idea. Byron would have shopped there. He loves all that campfire clothing. I'd just never met anyone like Danny, not in Rouyn, and I thought he was wonderful, wonderful enough to sleep with, which I had never done with anyone except Byron. But lately his ideas haven't looked too hot to me, and stenos hear things, too, and I knew he wasn't getting such a warm reception from agencies as he was telling me he was."

"Were you going to break it off, then?"

"I don't know. I wouldn't have let him down. But I don't know if I would have married him. Byron came home a couple of weeks ago for the weekend, and he's got a lot of good qualities I'd forgotten about, and then again I was glad when he went back up north. I guess I haven't found the right guy yet." Suddenly, as an aside, she said, "Maybe I expect too much." She resumed her tale. "So that's why I'm sad about Danny, but not laid out by it, in case you were wondering. What kind of man was he? This is what I've been trying to tell you. He was clever, but there was a lot of B.S. in him. He fooled himself, mostly, I think. You know what he was going to call the store? 'Nota Bene.'"

"What does that mean?"

"Footnote, doesn't it? In Latin. But if you pronounce it wrong it says 'not-a-Bean,' see? It reminds people of L. L. Bean because it's not-Bean, see. And it's also kind of a footnote to Bean."

"Was he planning to explain this to the customers if they didn't get it right away?"

She laughed. "I guess so."

"Did he ever talk about anything else he was involved with?"

"He never told me about anything. He was always being mysterious even about where he'd been for the last half hour if he was late. He used to hint that he was wheeling and dealing all over."

"In what?"

"He never said. I think it was mostly B.S."

"What about his life apart from you? Who were his friends?"

"He didn't have any. That's strange, isn't it? I don't have any myself, but I'm like that. Danny didn't have any and he should have. All men have friends, don't they?

Byron does. As soon as he comes off a survey they start calling each other up, getting together. Me and the boys and the beer, just like in the ad.''

"Was Pearson sexually active?"

"Huh?"

"With others. When your husband was in town. Did he have other women?"

"Oh, no. I'm pretty sure there was just me. Even with me, though it started with sex, for most of the time I was just an audience for him. I was surprised sometimes, well, how inactive he was. He was certainly different from Byron. I thought it went with his being intellectual. Made me think a bit."

Salter decided he needed a new topic. "Did he ever tell you any names of the people he was dealing with? Did you ever hear him on the phone using any?"

She came up with several Christian names she thought Pearson had used, and Salter made a list. Then he pushed the paper away. "Thanks, Mrs. Crouch. He didn't talk much about his affairs to you, did he?"

"Sure he did. He never stopped talking about this name generation thing, and the store." Her attitude said clearly that she would have been pleased if he had. "Come on, Inspector. Ask me what you want to know. I've only got an hour."

"Did he hate his wife?"

"No. Next question."

"Did she hate him?"

"I don't think so. She'd just had enough of him, that's all. It was just your average marriage breakdown. After a while she stopped being impressed by him, and then she found someone else. I expect he treated her badly, and that would be a big deal where she came from."

"What do you mean?"

"He had a bit of a temper. He probably hit her a couple of times."

"Did he ever hit you?"

"Heavens to Betsy, no. I wasn't his to hit. But I knew that might be a problem one day."

"But you were still going to marry him?"

"Maybe. But I can look after myself. I expect she couldn't."

Fascinated, unable to resist, Salter asked, "Do you get hit much now?"

"Me?" She stared at him. "By my husband? No, dummy. I told you, Byron's a dope, but he's not nasty with it." She paused. "The only thing is . . ." She shrugged and looked undecided.

"Yes?"

"I don't know about Danny's wife. I don't know about you, either, but, well, Danny liked to pretend to rape you sometimes. Not all the time. Maybe his wife got upset over that. You're supposed to. I don't mind. Byron likes to when he first comes back off a trip. All men do, I figure. Oh, well, maybe she's a feminist or something. I don't know. Anyway, that's all I can think of. Now I have to go."

"Thanks for being honest."

"I'm just trying to show you that you can find out everything I know by just asking me. Don't forget what I told you, I don't want you near my house, that's what I'm saying. If you believe me, you won't bother me."

"One last thing. Pearson used to work out of his apartment. Did you ever help him with that? The typing, maybe?"

"No way. We went to his place for fun. Besides, I never do people's typing, not even Byron's. It's one of the first rules of being a steno. Don't do people's typing in your spare time. There was nothing to keep me in his apartment once we'd done what we went there for." She waited a few moments, then said, "Now I have to go."

"Okay. Where can I find you if I want you?"

"At the office. Call me and I'll call you back. Okay?"

"It's possible that we may uncover something about Pearson that will make it necessary to bring you into it. Otherwise I'll try and leave you alone."

"What?" she said, sharply. "Like what?"

"I don't know at this point."

"Well, just be careful. You needn't bother to let me know what happens. I'll read about it in the papers." She rose and swung her purse strap over her shoulder. "Now I'm going."

TEN

THE INFORMATION that Madeline Crouch had provided had to be checked to give it any status. Salter had dealt with plenty of liars and Madeline Crouch seemed to him to be telling the truth, but she was sufficiently bizarre in her total poise for him to reserve judgment. He wanted to talk more to other people who had known Pearson, and he considered his choices. The most accessible source was still the bookstore. He checked his watch and drove over to Cumberland Avenue, where he parked outside Lilliput.

The store was open and Tommy Nystrom was sitting behind the cash register, reading a book. Nystrom looked up and performed a memory test on Salter. "The inspector," he said at last. "How are you, sir?"

Salter acknowledged the greeting and asked where Ruth Pearson was. Nystrom shook his head. "Not this week, old chap," he said. "We all figured the ghouls would be coming by to stare at her this week, so David and I are taking over while she hides. There's a girl who comes in on Fridays and Saturdays."

"Why not close the store?"

"It disrupts business too much. Not just loss of sales, but people suddenly not able to get hold of the store—salesmen and such."

"It's nice of you and Leese to find the time. Nice that you can, too."

"My time's my own and David's an academic. School's out now."

"Nice life."

"Me or David?"

"Both. What is it you do? Real estate?"

"I buy old houses and restore them and sell them for a huge profit. Sometimes I don't do a thing to them. Just sell them."

"For a profit?"

"Yes, it's amazing." Nystrom smiled. "Why? You have a house you want to sell?"

"No, but my wife wants to remodel us. Do you consult?"

"Where do you live?"

Salter told him.

"Solid burgher country that. It's hard to renovate north of Chaplin Crescent because they used a lot of gumwood in those parts and if you take that out there isn't much left. But, sure, I'll come up and look at it. Now, you didn't come here to talk about renovations. What can I do for you?"

Salter explained. He wanted to find out something about the Pearsons.

"What do you want to know?" Nystrom patted a chair beside the desk. "Park your bum on that while we chat," he added.

"For two people who were divorcing they seemed to be on pretty good terms," Salter said, sitting down.

"Weird, isn't it, or perhaps terribly modern. But don't forget that it's only recently they've known they were divorcing. Before that for a long time they were tippy-toeing around each other on little cats' feet."

"Why?"

"You're making me speak out of turn. Ruth is a friend of mine. Ask her."

"You might be able to save me a lot of trouble. I'd like to eliminate Mrs. Pearson as soon as possible."

"As a suspect? No way. She couldn't possibly do anything like that."

"Tell me why?"

"She wouldn't know how, for a start. Nor would she know where to ask. Most of all, though, the idea of Ruth killing anyone is grotesque."

"Too nice?"

"Of course she is. You've met her."

"Is that why she and Pearson were able to share the van and stuff, even though they had split up?"

"Yes. He called it being civilized, but it was just her nature. She still took messages for him, too. I told her to stay away from him."

"What is it to you? What do you care?"

"I care about Ruth. Because of David's wife she felt like the guilty party both with him and with her own husband, but I have no doubt that Pearson was having his toes licked by some adoring slave."

"That right? Who, do you think?"

"Who cares who? Somebody, you can be certain. Pearson was deeply in love with himself, but he needed to share his love. That was the role women played for him, admiring disciple."

"How do you know?"

"Ruth told me. It wasn't until David came along that she realized what a creep Pearson was. She wouldn't believe me when I told her. But David convinced her."

During all this Salter had been slightly puzzled, first by the nature of the relationship between Nystrom and Ruth Pearson, and then by the intimacy of it. "You and Mrs. Pearson are good friends, Mr. Nystrom?"

"Why?"

"I want to know if I can trust all this stuff."

"Oh, we're very close."

"Lovers?"

"Closer than that."

"Cousins? Brother and sister?"

Nystrom laughed. "Give up. You're not going to guess."

So tell me, thought Salter. But aloud, he said, "Do you know anything about Pearson's friends?"

"I never met any of his *chums*, Inspector. But I'll rack my brains and see if I can come up with anything."

"Thanks. Now what about you? You knew Pearson was going to use the van. You are a close friend of Mrs. Pearson, you say, very close. And of Leese's?"

"And of David's," Nystrom agreed.

"Then where were you on Saturday?"

Nystrom shook his head. "Struck out. I was here all day from noon onwards. I never left the store. I'd see the Princess some other time, I thought. Besides, I'd left my little Union Jack at home."

"Who can confirm that? That you never left the store, I mean?"

"David and Ruth. They were here most of the time and I was here when they weren't. And Ruth's part-time girl was here, too. She'll remember. I'm terribly mnemogenic."

Are you, thought Salter. He wasn't seriously questioning Nystrom, anyway. Just trying to sort out relationships around the bookstore.

The door opened and Leese appeared. "Ah, David, old love," Nystrom called. "Good. Now I must run. If you want me, Inspector, I'll be here every morning this week."

Leese moved behind the cash register and sat down. Salter waited for him to speak. Leese was silent, expectant. Curious, Salter walked to the window, looked at the ankles of the passersby on the sidewalk above for a few moments, then turned back to Leese, who continued to watch him in silence. It was becoming a contest.

Salter gave in. "Can we talk a bit more, Mr. Leese?"

"Certainly, now you've started."

"What do you mean?"

"I thought you might be one of those types who play no-speak games, and I'm determined not to lose to those buggers anymore."

"What are you talking about?"

"You must know them. You must work with them, in your business. There's a man I know—I've known him for twenty years—an academic, like me, lives not far away, near St. Clair and Yonge. Whenever I meet him, about once a week, on the street or on the subway platform, he stops as if I've called to him, and waits. And waits. And waits. And waits. For me to speak, that is. Remember, I didn't call out to him; I never do. I don't say a word. Just eye contact, that's all we start with. Now in the past I've *always* broken down and started babbling about the weather or Margaret Thatcher or something equally innocuous and he just nods, *interestedly*, as if that was why I stopped him. If I go on for a full two minutes he might say a word, and something like an ordinary human exchange would take place, and I can get away. So I decided not to do it anymore. Two weeks ago I met this bird on the Rosedale subway platform. We nodded and stood side by side while he waited for me to break down. I didn't, though. We got on the train. Still not a word. We sat down side by side and rode all the way down to Queen Street. Not a word. When I got off, suppressing the impulse to say even 'Ciao'—I did nod, though—he just watched me, *interestedly*. I caught him at it through the window as the train left. But I didn't lose. Nor will I. I can hold out as long as he can. So just now I thought you were one, but I see now you were just doing your inspector number. Very effective it is, too. Look at me babbling on. What do you want to know?"

"I want to know about Pearson."

"Ah. I am an authority on Ruth but not on Pearson, though I knew him a bit. I was grateful to him for agreeing to give up his wife without bloodshed, though he did want blood. Now I'm a prime suspect, I suppose. With Pearson alive, and with what my wife is demanding as the price of freedom, I would have been very hard up. As it is, we shall be all right."

"Who inherits?"

"He said, casually, eh, Inspector? I was wondering when you would slip that in. Ruth does. Every penny, including the insurance policies."

"So now you're in clover, right?"

"I don't know about that. Ruth is now feeling very guilty, and therefore, as any psychiatrist will tell you, I have become less attractive to her, not personally, but symbolically. Every time she looks at me she is reminded that her husband's death may be her fault, and a certain rejection of me takes place. It will be a while before we are normal."

"If you hadn't come along, would they still have separated?"

"Oh, yes. Ruth found her husband spooky."

"You agree? Just how well did you know him?"

"I met him a couple of times in the store before I took Ruth from him. Then afterwards, when he had heard about me, he insisted on getting together like civilized people, as he called it. He wanted half of everything, though."

"What would that have meant?"

"Ruth would have had to sell her house to give him half, plus his half of what the store was worth, or she would have had to sell the store to keep the house. Either way it would have been hard because my wife doesn't plan to leave me with much."

"But now you're all right."

"That's right. Now we're all right. It's a bad business, of course, but it had a good side for me, as you have already noted and underlined, Inspector."

There was a long pause. Salter said, "So tell me about him, would you?"

"Do you really want to know what I think? Or is this the newest technique for overhearing what *I'm* like?"

"For Christ's sake, Leese, just say the first thing that comes into your mind, will you?"

"Would we could return to such simplicity. Right, then. What do I think Pearson was like? First, I think he was driven by the need to fulfill his potential as he saw it. Everywhere he looked he saw lesser men, in his view, making it, and he was certain he could be making it, too. He was bright and personable—handsome, actually—and was once a successful salesman and then a manager of some kind. A junior executive, in fact. And there he stuck, because of course he was all form and no content. So he switched to advertising, within the same company, I think, and got a sniff of a whole new profession, then managed to get taken on by an agency. That didn't last long. He moved around a bit within the advertising world, then started his own production company for making television advertising and even, I think, toyed with the idea of making a real film, God help us. Then he found out about this name generation thing and then this latest venture, the clothing store. You understand that I pieced this all together from his conversation by inverting it, so to speak.

Pearson would begin a sentence with, 'When I was in advertising,' or the film business, or whatever, different sentences, you understand, I would translate that to 'Another failure of mine was in advertising.' Do I sound hard on him? Well, he gave Ruth a hard time. What separated them finally, I think, was her refusal to let him reorganize the bookshop. What he called her 'little shop' had made more money than he had for years, and he wanted to get into the act and thus undoubtedly screw it up. She had to threaten to close the store and reopen, on her own, in a different location unless he kept his hands off it. Again, you see, when he saw a successful business, he immediately saw how much more successful it would be with the benefit of his expertise. The word for him, I suppose, is entrepreneur. He *knew* that it was only lack of opportunity that prevented him from setting the world on fire, and he was always looking for an opportunity. A touch of the Zimri.''

''A what?''

''A man in a poem by Dryden. 'Was everything by starts and nothing long.' Not really appropriate, though, because as I remember it Zimri was a joke, but I didn't find Pearson very funny at all. He also liked to rub shoulders with the movers and shakers—he dressed the part, certainly. He reminded me sometimes of a barber who was aping his rich clients. The world had gone to Pearson's head. His public persona was that of a warm, genial, successful guy, on terms with the world. After he found out I was an academic, he wanted to talk to me about Plato. He had totally lost interest in Ruth, if he was ever interested in her as a person, but in public he affected a fond attitude to his 'little Ruthie.' The difference between the public and private man scared her eventually.''

''Did he have enemies?''

"You know he should have, because he was unscrupulous, or wanted to be, but I think he was never in a position to do much damage. The thing is, I believe that he couldn't conceal himself long enough to get trusted. Do you know what I mean? People got a malodorous whiff from him and sheered away."

"He was a failure, then?"

"Yes, in his own terms, certainly. But he hadn't given up hope. He believed in that store he wanted to start. He had three enemies: Ruth, me, and Tommy Nystrom. We all knew him like nobody else, and we all wanted him to go away, far away. While he was in a position to harm Ruth, we stayed civil. But we watched him. Like a hawk, in my case."

"Now everything's dandy, isn't it?"

"What's this, Salter's fork? If I say yes, it looks suspicious. If I say no, after telling you how little I loved the departed, it looks hypocritical, and therefore, again, suspicious. Of course it's dandy now. Pearson's death does not diminish me in the slightest. For Ruth, and therefore for me, it's like winning a lottery. My reaction to the news was first pleasure, then shock."

Leese stopped with an air of finality and Salter looked for another button to press. "Tell me what spooky means. You say Mrs. Pearson found him spooky."

"I chose the word with care. Pearson made her uneasy. She had begun to feel for a long time that there was a dimension of him she knew nothing about. A touch of the Jekyll and Hyde is how she described it to me. To put it simply, she woke up one day and realized he gave her the creeps, that she was slightly afraid of him, and she wanted him to go away. She put it to me that she found him a bit inhuman. I thought she had just heard the hollow at the core. But now she feels guilty because she thinks she may have been an inadequate wife from the start."

Salter took in all this without judging it, reflecting how rarely police work involved dealing with verbal types like Leese, and in the end how rarely their eloquence illuminated anything. He could imagine the difficulty of presenting a jury a killer's motives in the kind of terms Leese was using, and what fun the two opposing sets of psychiatrists would have arguing the case. When all was said, what he wanted was a simple motive, some fingerprints, three witnesses, and a confession. He prodded Leese on.

"Mrs. Pearson said he had a vicious side. Someone else said the same thing," he said.

"I would think women would know more about that than men, but I got a taste of it once. The last time he was fired I ran into him in the café next door, and all his old Sunny Jim, my-friend-the-philosopher side was gone. What I got instead was a diatribe about people in academic life who know nothing about the real world. Conventional enough stuff, we get it all the time—you must get it, too, you're paid by the taxpayer—but he articulated it with some venom.

"Normally I find it easy to respond to that kind of stuff. What do they mean by the real world? I live in it. I've experienced birth, and love, and I expect to die. I pay taxes. I suffer. Do I not bleed? I generally wind up asking them what they mean by the real world, and when did they last kill their own dinner. What, after all, is real about making commercials for male beauty products? Harder than teaching Canadians to speak French? But I mustn't go on. I'll get angry." Leese stopped. He had delivered all this in a voice over which he had so much control that at the end he was beginning to stammer. He took a large swallow. "Yes, I think you could say I agree with Ruth," he ended in a parody of a man speaking in measured language. Leese's speech sounded rehearsed to Salter; not a solid demonstration of Pearson's peculiar viciousness but the defensive reaction of an academic whenever the "real world" is invoked.

He changed the subject. "Mr. Nystrom tells me you can confirm he was in the store on Saturday."

"I can indeed. He never left it." Leese was still angry.

Salter said, "He's very close to Mrs. Pearson, isn't he?"

"He is, indeed."

"What's going on?" Salter asked, suddenly. "Is this some kind of troika?" A crude, battering question sometimes produced quick results. This one did.

"In the name of Christ, what are you talking about?" Leese said with such fury that Salter froze slightly, watching for some physical move.

Leese continued. He spread out his hand and ticked the points off on his fingers. "Facts of life," he said. "One: Ruth Pearson is in love with me. Two: I am in love with Ruth Pearson. Three: Tommy Nystrom is Ruth Pearson's greatest friend. Four: I don't mind that because, five: Tommy Nystrom is homosexual and lives in a tree house somewhere with his friend. Any more?"

"Yes. What are you shouting for?"

Leese swelled for a few moments, then collapsed with a huge sigh. "I wasn't, actually, shouting, but you're right. It comes from thinking about Pearson. Sorry. Right. Let me tell you about Ruth and Nystrom, without invading their privacy. They've been friends for more than twenty years. In the past they've helped each other through some difficult times. She went through some sort of spiritual crisis at university, joined one of those intellectual Christian gangs, and he just waited around until she got over it and was there when she emerged, whereas everyone else had given her up, including her family. In turn, when his crisis came, she held his hand. It's a bond thicker than blood or sex, I'll tell you. I'm slightly jealous of it. Who isn't jealous of being on the outside of a relationship that is apparently so, what, profound? But I like Tommy.''

They were interrupted at this point by a customer, and Salter took his leave. So long as Leese was flowing, he wanted to listen, but he had no more questions of his own. It was an opportunity to have a look at Ranovic doing his impersonation of a street trader.

ELEVEN

SALTER FOUND HIM selling his postcards outside the Holt, Renfrew store. The undercover man was leaning against the wall, watching people look over his stock, apparently indifferent to his customers. From the edge of the sidewalk, Salter watched for a few minutes and realized that Ranovic's expression went beyond boredom. The man looked broken-hearted. Salter looked along the row of traders and saw that Rosie Porlock had seen him and was even then telling George Miner, who was stroking his face hair and looking at Salter. Salter considered his problem. Ranovic was asking for help; if this were a movie he would simply order up a wagon, and two uniformed men would grab Ranovic and take him into custody where they could talk in peace. Salter figured that it would take him an hour to set it up and probably require two requisitions, signed by a more senior officer. In the end, he distanced himself as far as he could from the peddlers, and called Miner over. "Where are your pals?" he asked. "The others I talked to on Sunday?"

"I don't know, sir. You could try the front of the Hudson's Bay store."

"Would the other two know?" Salter indicated Rosie Porlock and Ranovic.

Miner shrugged and Salter nodded to release him. He beckoned Rosie over next and put the same question to her. She suggested Yonge Street, by the Eaton Centre. Then he called Ranovic over.

"What's the problem?" he asked.

"I've been fingered," Ranovic said. "I'm finished."

"You mean these peddlers know you're a cop? Okay, so I'll take you off. I told you. I thought they had."

"Not *these* people. The dealers out on my regular turf."

There was no room to discuss Ranovic's problem under the eyes of Rosie and George Miner, and Salter had only half an idea of what Ranovic was saying. But there was no doubt that it was serious.

"So tell me what to do," Salter said. "You want off this job? Is it dangerous?"

But Ranovic acted like a man who has been gutted, unable to find the energy to reply. "Not here," he said eventually. "Not this stuff."

"Stay here for the afternoon, then. Okay. Or quit. Whatever you want. No, stay here for the afternoon and meet me in the office at six. By the way, I'm supposed to be asking you where the other three peddlers are. You don't know. Okay?"

Ranovic shrugged and went back to his stand, which Salter assumed meant he agreed.

AMONG PEARSON'S PAPERS concerning his name-generating activities, Salter had come across the names of two people in agencies who had given Pearson work. When he called on one of them, it turned out that the two knew each other, so Salter arranged to meet them both in one of the local pubs. He did not expect much, but they were the only work contacts of Pearson he could find.

He inquired at the bar of the Prince Arthur Lounge and was directed to two men sitting at a table by the window overlooking Avenue Road. They rose to meet him and shook hands with him in turn. One of them, Bob Blake, was a big man with the air of a sometime athlete, in his forties, with short gray hair and steel-rimmed glasses, and an enveloping handshake. The other, Jack Hines, was more like what Salter had thought an advertising man would look like. Also about forty, his hair was fashionably styled, like an English schoolboy's. He wore what seemed to be a series of blouses, a fawn one next to his skin and a dark brown one, with a lot of pockets, over the top. His pants were creamy balloons, pegged at the ankle, where they met a pair of canvas boots. Salter sat down and ordered a beer. He started in immediately. "I want to know who killed your friend Pearson. When I went through his papers your names cropped up a lot. So maybe you can tell me something about Pearson. No one else can. Let's start with you, Mr. Blake. Was he a friend of yours?"

Blake shook his head. "No. He sold ideas to my company."

"Names?"

Blake nodded. "That's right. And I played tennis with him sometimes, during the winter."

"Why only the winter?"

"In the summer we both played regularly at different outdoor clubs. But during the winter we both belonged to the same downtown club, and we played every other week. Not on a regular basis, but pretty frequently."

"What kind of man was he? Did you like him?"

"Not enough to want to see him after hours, except for tennis. I liked playing with him well enough; he was very classical—had all the proper shots—so you got a good game, win or lose. But I didn't like him."

"Why?"

"He was a prick. He's dead now, and I'm sorry, but that's what he was. He was the kind of guy who if he saw you waiting for his space in a parking lot would keep you waiting another ten minutes while he read his diary. Stuff like that, never letting anyone in ahead of him in heavy traffic."

"Apart from driving what was he like?"

Blake laughed. "What's anyone like apart from driving? That's how you tell about people. Have you noticed, by the way, that the new thugs on the road, the bullies, are all young professional women showing they've got balls now, like seventeen-year-old kids did with their first car."

Another one, thought Salter. He took a long pull of his drink. "What do you know about him privately, when he was out of a car?" He addressed the question to both of them. "Was he a drunk? Did he gamble? Did he use whores?"

"He didn't drink much."

"He was no gambler," Blake said. "I saw him at a stag once—you know the kind where there's a poker game and ten percent of every pot goes to the groom. He was bored stiff. Didn't even know the rules of poker."

"Women?"

The two men exchanged glances but not in a way that was intended to fool Salter. It was like the look between actors just before they take a bow together.

"We think he might have been a little weird," Blake said. "You know his marriage broke down? We never saw or heard of a sign of another woman."

"You know any *men* he made a pass at?"

"No, but . . ."

"Then what are you talking about?"

Blake shrugged. "He kept his private life very private."

"Tell me something else about him."

"There's nothing else." Blake looked at Hines significantly. Hines said, "The man should know, Bob," with an air of solemnity. There was a long silence. Then Blake said, or rather mouthed, silently, "Grass." Then he added, "He supplied."

"He was a dealer?" Salter asked. "Anything else besides marijuana?"

"No!" Blake jerked back in an alarmed recoil.

"That you know of, anyway. He supplied you two, did he? Anybody else you know?"

Hines shook his head quickly, more, Salter thought, as a signal to Blake than a reply to him. "So for all you know he just slipped a little to you two. Did he get any work from both of you?"

Both men nodded.

"Then I suspect he was just doing you a favor, a perk, like supplying you with a call girl to say thank you for the business. Did you pay him for the stuff he brought you?"

"Damn right," Blake said. "We paid the full price."

"Okay. Thanks." Salter stood up. "I probably won't be in touch."

The two men needed to talk to each other, and Salter left them there and went back to his office to hear about Ranovic's troubles.

"I'VE BEEN FINGERED," Ranovic said once more, as soon as they were settled in Salter's office.

"So you said. What does that mean?"

"It means I'm finished, doesn't it." The tone made the question rhetorical. Ranovic's emotion was hard to respond to. He was not asking for answers, but, slightly dramatically it seemed to Salter, verbalizing his despair and adding a dash of irritation at Salter for not immediately understanding and communing. Patiently Salter waited for Ranovic's mind to overtake his emotions. It was like dealing with someone much younger, a child even, who has suffered his first major disappointment.

"Who was it?"

"Who was it? Colley Laker, that's who it was."

"Tell me who Colley Laker is."

Sighing, Ranovic explained. "Colley Laker is my source. The rounder I buy from."

Salter waited.

"Do you know what I do? How I work?" Now there was some hostility in Ranovic's tone. Salter ignored it and made a "tell me" gesture.

"I am the man in place at the Lake Simcoe Hotel. That's where the out-of-town bikers meet up with the West End crowd. The dealers. Colley Laker is a dealer. As far as he knew, until today I was a little operator. But I bought grass from him and I reported back here. My job was to supply information. Somewhere in this building—" Ranovic pointed contemptuously upwards "—they put it all together and figured out who the big boys were. That was the idea, anyway. With enough guys like me phoning in the information they could start to see a pattern, maybe intercept the next big shipment. I don't know. That was my job—buy from Colley Laker and tell the people here who he mixed with, when he came and went, stuff like that."

"So what happened?"

"Colley Laker saw me today on Bloor Street, peddling postcards. It was always a chance, but I figured not a big one."

"Couldn't you be doing that and dealing a little?"

"Colley doesn't think so. Not deal out of the West End, anyway. So he took a good long look at me, and you could see him putting two and two together. Then he came back a couple of hours later with Bomber Steele."

"Who is . . . ?"

"Bomber Steele is an enforcer. He breaks legs. He got the name somewhere years ago in the fight game. So the two of them stood there while Laker made a fucking pantomime of pointing me out to the Bomber, who nods a couple of times, slowly.''

Ranovic stopped and began to gather himself together like a man who has finished what he was to say. "Then what?" Salter asked.

"That's it. Then they left. I got the message."

"We can protect you."

"You don't have to protect me. They won't touch me as long as I carry on selling postcards. The message was—that's it, copper, don't come our way again."

"You mean they saw you selling postcards and figured out you're working undercover on Bloor Street?"

"Sound farfetched? These guys aren't stupid, you know. No. I think it means they've been suspicious of me for a long time, and someone told Colley Laker that I was hanging around the area after the bombing. Maybe they saw you and me talking, I don't know. But Colley Laker came down today to take a look at me, and then he sent for the Bomber. You could say I'm lucky."

"Why can't you go back on the squad, in some other district? What would happen?"

"Are you kidding? Bomber is what would happen. The last time they caught an undercover man they broke two arms and a leg. I've had a warning. With me it would be both legs. At least. I'm finished."

"On the drug squad, maybe. But, Christ, there's other kinds of work."

"Yeah? Giving out tickets? Court duty?"

"We've all done it."

"I know. I didn't, though, and I don't want to. I got taken on to undercover work right off the training course. I don't even know where my uniform is." Ranovic was calming down now, hardly dramatizing himself at all.

"Is the drug squad that much fun?" Salter asked.

"It's terrific. Like being a spy. Stressful as hell, of course, and a lot of guys crack. Maybe everyone does eventually, but I was still getting a charge out of it. You know those spy novels, the good ones, I mean, they tell it how it is. I mean, like, *The Spy Who Came in from the Cold*. About the way it is out there, all by yourself, trying not to make a false move. But the one thing I've never read about is how exciting it is. I went for months being Bruno Caroli."

"They used to write stories about that side," Salter said. "I read them as a kid." He wondered if he mentioned Bulldog Drummond whether Ranovic would have heard of him, and then decided not to risk it. At the same time he was feeling ironic about Bruno Caroli he was feeling sorry for Gorgi Ranovic. "I don't know what to tell you," he said. "I don't know anything about your world, though I know what it's like to have the rug taken from under you. Why don't you finish this job with me and see what happens? It's not a bad job even in uniform. I thought it was pretty good at your age."

"That was during the Depression, wasn't it? Okay, sorry. Sure. What next, then?"

Salter picked up a message that was on his desk. "They've found Pearson's car," he said. "In the municipal garage on Cumberland between Bay and Yonge. Go and take a look at it. It's in the basement. Then tell the police garage to put it away. Hold on. Maybe these guys insured themselves. The bomb squad should look at it first, shouldn't they?"

"I'll meet them there. Let me look after it. Do we have keys?"

"I don't know if it's on the ring they gave me. Here. If not, break in."

"Okay. I'll call you."

"Call me at home if you find anything interesting."

The last item Salter had to deal with before he went home was a report from Constable Brennan, who had been waiting patiently to deliver it since Salter arrived. When he called him in, Brennan opened his notebook and began. He gave the date and time and said, "First I interviewed the officers on duty in the garage between Cumberland Street and Yorkville Avenue on the afternoon of the incident."

Salter said, "Leave the notebook with me. I'll read it and sign it tomorrow. Just tell me what you did. What did the police in the garage say?"

"What about?"

"Whatever you *asked* them."

"I asked them what time the garage was sealed off on the Saturday morning and what time it reopened. They closed it at nine hundred and reopened it at approximately fourteen forty-five."

"I know. I was there. Did they have anything to say?"

"They said they had been able to keep every level of the garage under observation all day, and no one had been on foot in the garage while it was closed."

All this Salter knew, but he didn't want to squelch Brennan further. "How many police were covering the garage?"

"Six. They were strategically posted to keep the whole garage under surveillance."

"Good. Who else have you spoken to?"

Brennan went down the list. Every storekeeper and assistant within view of the garage on both sides. He had been very thorough, but the result was a blank.

"That's the street level done, then," Salter said. "What about the upper levels? There are a lot of second- and third-floor stores on both those streets."

"I'll start those tomorrow."

Salter nodded encouragingly. "You probably won't find anyone who saw anything at all. Not the first round anyway. But finish them up. The fact that no one saw anything is just as important as finding someone who thinks he saw something, just not so exciting. It's got to be done." He released Brennan, who left looking slightly more cheerful, and went home.

THAT NIGHT Ranovic called his house to report that he had found two pounds of Acapulco gold in the trunk of Pearson's car.

TWELVE

"Two POUNDS of Acapulco is expensive," Ranovic said. "I think it makes him some kind of dealer."

They were in Salter's office the next morning.

"I know he was supplying some guys in advertising. Probably for business favors, the way they used to supply girls. They claimed they paid him, but I have my doubts."

"Yeah? But this was a little more, I would guess. I didn't see any butts around his apartment, so I don't think he smoked himself. Two pounds of Acapulco is the real shit, you know. But I don't think it's a living."

"I think I can check if he smoked himself. But where would he get it?"

"Any one of three hundred places. I could name you twenty. You want me to find out? Someone in the squad might know."

"How much did you use to buy?"

"Two, three pounds. But not this stuff. This is the real shit."

"So you said. Did you sell it?"

"You mean in bags, like? Nah. I should've. I like selling. I should have been a street trader. Really."

Ranovic was obviously feeling better about himself, and Salter let the business slide for a few moments. "Why didn't you?"

"Listen, my family is not very proud of me being a cop. Where we come from cops are—well—my grandfather was a big man in Dubrovnik. My father had two degrees before he left to come over here. So he wasn't too keen about me joining the force. But street trading would be worse. Like being a ragpicker or something. What they'd really like is for me to become a lawyer."

"So tell me how you can find out about Pearson?"

"He would have got the stuff from the bikers or one of the rounders, like Colley Laker. Probably a rounder operating out of one of the bars near here. If we're lucky, it'll be someone we've got our eye on."

"You watch these guys all the time?"

"Enough so we get to know the customers. Give me a picture and I'll see what I can do. I'll pass it on to my boss and he can see if any of our boys recognizes him."

Salter made a note on his desk pad. "What did you do with the stuff you bought?"

Ranovic became round-eyed. "Oh, I deposited it with my boss. Most of it. Why?" He was grinning as he spoke.

"I shouldn't have asked." Salter changed the topic. "Have you thought any more about what you do next? It had to happen sometime, didn't it?"

"I guess so. I'm giving it some thought. I may have trouble coming back. That's the real risk in this work. Crossing over. When you go under you have to really get into it, think of yourself as a dealer. Live the life. It can happen that you can't come back over."

" 'Surface,' you mean. If you go 'under' then you have to 'come up,' don't you, not 'cross over'?"

"Huh? I guess so. But 'crossing over' is what they call it."

Salter let it drop. "What do you mean, anyway? Why can't you come back over?"

"Like one guy I knew. He went under and rented a real stinkhole in Chinatown. Dealt a little for cover, got himself a girlfriend off the street, she lived with him in this real scuzzy room, helped him deal, like, you know, helped out in the shop? She never knew he was a cop. What happened was that he stopped looking after himself so they tried to reassign him, but he quit and disappeared. I don't know what happened to him next, but I'd guess he's a dealer in Montreal or someplace. I know how he felt."

"You think you'll quit?"

"I don't know. I like the force, but the guy I'll probably be working for after this, he likes you to be tidy, you know?"

Salter took in the black tangle of Ranovic's hair. It would look strange under a police cap. He stood up. "You want to know what it was like when I joined?" He was still smarting from Ranovic's crack that he had joined during the Depression.

"Yeah, but you guys. You were lucky to get in, weren't you? I mean with guys riding freight trains, looking for any kind of job."

God help us, thought Salter. He wasn't joking. Twenty years, fifty years, it's all the same history to his generation. "I miss the old pointed helmets, though," he said. "They were real good for storing stuff under."

"Is that right?" Ranovic said, respectful, puzzled.

"I'm joking," Salter said so that Ranovic would not repeat the story outside the office. It was like making fun of a child. "Did you brush up against the mob when you were working in the West End?"

"Oh, sure, but I didn't always know it. The big dealers, the bikers, the mob, it's all connected and, like I told you, there are guys in this building as well as the horsemen over in the Kremlin on Jarvis Street trying to figure out *how* they are connected. I was part of the intelligence, but they didn't tell me what they knew. Our people, I mean."

"Does this bombing look like something the mob would do?"

"You'll have to ask Organized Crime about that. Doesn't the mob generally use plastique?"

"They use contract killers who use what they like, I hear. They use the bikers, too, don't they?"

"You're asking the wrong guy. I just know about dealing. Talk to Danny de Angelis. He's the one who knows how the mob works. But what would the mob want to blow this guy up for? They're businessmen, not cowboys."

DANNY DE ANGELIS was a civilian, a graduate in criminology who, at thirty, still dressed like a graduate student in blue jeans and a red shirt with collar buttons. He was making a career out of understanding the workings of organized crime in Canada. He had the most books in his room that Salter had ever seen in a police office, all of them concerning the activities of organized crime in Canada and the U.S.A. As well, he had four file cabinets packed with press clippings. The leading gangsters did not know him to see him, although they were aware that someone like de Angelis was thinking about them all the time. De Angelis had worked on understanding organized crime for long enough so that he was able, as he put it, to "think mob thoughts" wherever something that might touch on the activities of the mob was involved.

"They wouldn't have any interest in this thing the way you've described it," he told Salter. "There's always a good business reason why the mob gets interested. This bookstore? Was it maybe standing in the way of some deal they were putting together? Has the dead guy's wife heard of anyone who wants to buy out her lease? And the mob isn't into organizing street traders yet, so there's nothing there. This guy—what did you say he was? A name generator? How would that interest them? Sure there's a threat and a bomb, but it sounds like a crank to me. All the same, whoever did it had to know how to rig it, so I'll see if there's anything in the pipeline. Sometimes we get a tip, very unofficial, that keeps us straight. They don't like to be blamed for everything. I'll find out if there's any whisper of a pro around, and if there's one the mob hasn't hired they might know about him and send us a message. You can never trust them, of course, but sometimes we've been making inquiries, talking to known mobsters, and then a piece of information comes down that we can check out. I'll let you know."

A CALL TO MADELINE CROUCH confirmed one point. "You don't have to come down," he said. "Just a quick question. Did Pearson smoke grass?"

"You mean marijuana?" She pronounced it with a naïve intonation—"mar*u*wana." "Never. Not while I was around."

THAT EVENING, as Salter was replacing a light bulb over the front door, Tommy Nystrom appeared. Salter stared at him, wondering where he had seen him before.

"Tommy Nystrom. Lilliput," the man said.

"Oh. Yeah. Hi." Salter said.

"I was in the neighborhood, looking at a house on Duplex, and I remembered you saying you lived here, so I drove down the avenue and there you were, being domestic."

"That's right," Salter said. So what? Or, rather, now what?

"You want me to look at your house. You are going to renovate it. Remember?"

"Oh, yes. I'm sorry." It was seeing Nystrom away from the investigation that had taken Salter by surprise. The habit learned in school of keeping the worlds of home and work strictly apart had stayed with Salter and it was always a surprise when a character from one world appeared in the other. "Come in," he said. He called out, "Annie?" By the time the two men had walked through the kitchen, Annie had appeared from the garden. "I told Mr. Nystrom here we were thinking of remodeling. He offered to have a look, tell us what he thought. He does this for a living."

Annie, who was used not merely to taking the lead in any household arrangements but to dragging Salter around on her back whenever she wanted some part of the house painted or repaired, was registering amazement that her tentative and barely formed wish for a new interior for the house had been turned so quickly into a figure in the living room, ready to advise.

"But I don't know what I want to do yet," she said.

Nystrom smiled at her. "Use me for a sounding board. Maybe that's all I will be good for."

"Want a beer?" Salter asked.

"No, thanks." Nystrom put back his head and sniffed. "Coffee? Is there some left?"

"I'll make some more," Annie offered.

"I'll have a look out back while the water's boiling." Nystrom disappeared through the door into the garden.

"Where did he come from?" Annie asked as soon as he was out of earshot.

"He's a friend of the woman whose husband was blown up. The bookshop owner."

"Is he an architect?"

"He said he remodels houses and sells them. He's not charging anything to look. It's a favor. A perk. He wants to keep in with the cops."

Nystrom returned as Annie was setting out the coffee cups. "What's the problem?" he asked. "What do you want to do?"

"It's gloomy in here," Annie said. "Cozy in the winter, but gloomy in the summer."

"Where, particularly?"

"In the kitchen."

"You need a new kitchen, anyway," Nystrom said. "You can't do much else about a house like this. It's well-built, badly designed, and ugly. If you really don't like it, I would move, because there are people who like this kind of thing. Why not sell it, and find something more..." He waved his hands. "Less *heavy*," he concluded.

"Good," Annie said. "That's what I want to do."

"Oh, terrific," Salter said, gloomily.

"You don't have to help," Annie said. "I'll find a place."

"So everybody's happy," Nystrom said. "Wonderful. My fee is another cup of coffee."

The doorbell rang and Annie went to answer it.

"Any news of the mad bomber yet?" Nystrom asked. "Or shouldn't I be asking?"

"We have a number of leads," Salter said.

Nystrom burst out laughing. "You really say that."

"Tell me some more about Pearson," Salter said, ignoring Nystrom's glee. "What did you know about him? What kind of guy was he? Why did he break up with his wife? Why does he seem to have had no friends? What did he do in his spare time?"

"To start with the last first. I don't think he had what you and I would call spare time," Nystrom said. "He worked all the time. All he cared about was making it. Getting rich somehow."

"But this store of his. Wasn't it a kind of retirement project?"

"Oh, no. Just another scheme. He was involved constantly in schemes. He had no time for friends. He had business associates."

"No private life at all?"

"Women, you mean? I don't know if there were any. But *I* wouldn't have heard if there were."

He seemed to be inviting further questions but Salter knew more answers than Nystrom did on the subject. "You didn't like him much, did you?" he asked.

Nystrom shrugged. "No, but that didn't cause any problems because I didn't have to deal with him."

"You're a good friend of his wife's, though."

"Yes, I am. I predate David and I predate the late Mr. Pearson. Ruth is about my oldest friend. We need each other."

Salter hardly noticed the speed at which they had arrived at such a nakedness. Nystrom was making him feel stupid.

"Have you eliminated the traders yet?" Nystrom asked.

The question made clear to Salter why Nystrom had "dropped by." He considered his reply carefully. "You can't eliminate anyone until you've charged someone else," he said, making it sound like a message.

"They seem harmless enough, though."

The man was still fishing, and Salter decided to change the subject by doing a little fishing himself. "Do you handle stores as well as houses?" he asked.

"I might if the whole building were for sale. I haven't yet."

"What would it cost to set up a store in Yorkville? If I wanted to set up my wife like Ruth Pearson?"

"Ruth started with a thousand. I think she took out a tiny mortgage. But that was fifteen years ago when the rent was a hundred and twenty-five a month."

"What is it now?"

"About two thousand. It'll be three when her lease comes up for renewal."

"So what would it cost to start now?"

"A bookshop? Fifty thousand. If the publishers gave you lots of credit."

"What about something like a clothing store?"

"A hundred thousand. Why? What does she want to sell?"

"Isn't there anywhere cheaper? What about Yonge Street, say, north of Eglinton?"

"Rents up there are as high as Yorkville. Your best bet would be to get her a street trader's license. You could help out Saturday afternoons. But doesn't your wife work now?"

Salter was saved from responding to this by the arrival of Annie from the front of the house. Nystrom greeted her with an enthusiasm that made Salter feel he had been boring him for hours.

"I've had an inspiration," Nystrom said. "Stay here and put your kitchen in the front of the house. You can watch the street while you string beans. Make this space the dining room."

"You can't have a kitchen in the *front*," Salter protested.

The other two laughed and Salter shut up.

For another fifteen minutes, while Salter watched them in silence, Annie and Nystrom rearranged his house. Then, as it seemed to Salter, Nystrom revolved three times and spun away in a cloud of smoke. In fact, Nystrom merely looked at his watch, shook hands with them both at the same time, promised Annie he would think about textures for her, and left, through the front door.

"Where did you meet him?" Annie asked, still crackling from the energy Nystrom had brought with him.

"I told you. He's a friend of the dead man's widow. I told him we were thinking of remodeling. He fixes houses. I didn't arrange for him to come."

"Then why did he?"

"He said he was just passing, but he sure wants to find out how the case is going. I would, too, if I were him. But, as I said, he won't be charging us anything."

"You think he's mixed up in this bombing thing?"

Salter thought about this. "I think he's mixing himself up in it. He may just be dying of curiosity, but most people stay right out of the way when we're on a case. But if you're asking me if I think he did it, then, no. Now let's have a beer."

"Phone your father first."

"Oh, shit. What now?"

"Don't panic. He sounds happy about something. He even asked me how I was."

Nevertheless Salter armed himself with a beer before he dialed the number.

"It's Seth," the old man said. "He's just left, so I thought I'd give you a call, tell you what he's up to now."

"I'm sorry, Dad. He just wants to be helpful. It's a stage he's going through. But I'll tell him to lay off."

"No, no. Don't do that. You know what he's doing?"

"What he was doing before, I guess. Trying to be a good grandson. I'll make him stop."

"No, I don't want that. He's on to something else now. Didn't he tell you?"

"No, he's very secretive. What's he up to?"

"He wants to do my oral history."

"What's that?"

"My oral history. Hold on. Is that right, May? Yes, that's right. Oral history. He's got a recording machine and he wants me to tell him my history. We did a bit of it already this afternoon."

"You mean the story of your life?"

"That's it. He wants to take it all down. On tape."

"Do you mind?"

"No, I don't mind. Not really. It's a bit interesting, in a way, hearing yourself. But here's the thing, see." There was a pause. "Should I say everything? About me and your mother and the old days in Cabbagetown? I don't know how much you've told him about all that. Should I skip over anything?"

It took Salter a minute to realize what his father was saying, which was, roughly, in marrying above himself, had Salter concealed his past in any way, and should the old man keep quiet about it? An image flashed on Salter's mind, a Hollywood movie of the thirties: the young hypocrite leaving the society church on the arm of the heiress and there in the crowd, his worthy old anonymous parents, standing, clean as new pins, weeping happily at their son's good fortune, then sadly as they walk back to their hovel after the limousine has departed. Or was it Pip when Joe Gargery comes to call? It was unbelievable, but what else could the old man be talking about? "Tell him everything you can remember, Dad," he said. "Everything. I'll pay for the tapes. Okay? No, wait. Don't tell about the time you caught me in the woodshed with those other kids. Nor about the time I stole the holiday money from Mum's purse."

"What are you talking about? I don't remember anything about any woodshed. And you never stole a cent from anybody in your life. Not a cent."

"I must be remembering someone else. Okay, enjoy yourself, then."

When Seth came home and said nothing, Salter, too, kept quiet. He saved it for Annie, in bed, who was enchanted with the whole story and agreed that the powerful respectability censor in the old man's head had already done all the necessary editing. She further pointed out what Salter might have perceived long since, that a lot of the old man's crankiness in the presence of his son's family probably stemmed from the permanent tension he was under not to let his son down in polite society.

THIRTEEN

"YOU'RE PROBABLY RIGHT," Orliff said. "You've established that this guy was dealing a little grass, so he mixed in rough company. Given the method, it makes sense. As for the rest, you've ruled out the wife and the two boyfriends. And you think the traders are harmless. It all makes sense. Let's pass it on."

"What happens then?"

"Homicide will pick it up."

"And they'll start all over again, won't they?"

"Probably. But, look, I know I told you this was a bad time to get a case you couldn't solve, but that isn't such a serious concern now. That's enough. Write up the report."

But it wasn't enough. Salter was beginning to feel his neck. He had made an assumption that Pearson was the key, and he was running out of time before he could prove it. He had early on discounted the bookstore trio, but he had not cleared them to the satisfaction of anyone coming fresh to the case. Orliff, unusually relaxed as he faced his retirement, was taking his investigation on trust, but even he would be dismayed by Salter's lack of thoroughness. He had brushed aside the traders, too, on the strength of Ranovic's assurances and his own instincts, and this aspect of the investigation was also looking cursory. Unless he could find the answer, or completely clear the bookstore trio and the street traders, he was going to look bad. All he had done so far was increase the probability that he was right. It was too late now to do anything about the traders, but something more might be done about the bookstore people. He decided to take a new direction, to assume that one (or two) of the bookstore trio was responsible, and try to prove it. If he failed, it might help a little when he handed the case over.

"Let me use the time we've got left," he asked Orliff.

Orliff looked irritated. "What else have you got to try?"

"His drug connections, for one. Ranovic hasn't finished working on that yet."

"You think you could find anything out? Those guys are cute."

"I don't know. Then there are the original threatening letters. I want to think some more about them." Salter was scrambling now, trying to sound like a man with a genuine idea. "The laboratory said they were written on two different typewriters. I want to think about that."

Orliff sucked a hollow tooth, unengaged in Salter's quest. "The guy's dead," he said. "But keep me posted." He looked at a letter on his desk. "The news will be out any day, by the way."

"News about what?"

"My replacement. Don't you care anymore? Never mind asking me. Wait and see."

RANOVIC REPORTED in the next afternoon.

"Pearson was one of Sticky Newton's customers," he announced.

"That explains everything. Who the hell is Sticky Newton?"

"Beggin' yo pardin, sorr," Ranovic said in an absurd parody of an Irish accent. "You really are in administration, aren't you? Sticky Newton is a rounder." He paused.

"I know what a rounder is. Get on with it."

"Right. Sticky Newton has been under observation for a long time because we're trying to get something big on him. But we haven't made anything stick yet. That's not why he's called Sticky, by the way. He got that name in his early shoplifting days when everything stuck to his fingers on the way through the store."

"Tell me about his childhood, too."

"Yes. Right. Sorry." Ranovic sat up smartly. "Sticky Newton operates out of the Granada Tavern—that's off Bloor Street. He's the supplier for the district, we think, and we think he's connected."

"Who to? Who's we?"

"The drug squad. We think he's connected to a big source, or one of them."

"He'd have to be, wouldn't he, unless he grows the stuff."

"Not really. He could be getting it from another rounder, but we think he gets it from a source. We've been watching him for six months. We've tried to nail him for selling it, but he's cute. He never has the stuff on him, or in his car, and he wouldn't keep any in his apartment. He's got a penthouse, by the way, on Bloor Street. So we've been watching. We know some small traders buy from him—two-bit stuff, but we weren't sure how he delivered. We've seen Pearson talking to him in the tavern. By the way, Newton hasn't been seen since the bombing, but that always happens when there's any trouble. It doesn't mean anything except it confirms, probably, that Pearson was a regular customer."

"Now tell me why they would kill him."

"The best answer is money. If Pearson was stupid, he tried to cross Newton, took delivery, and didn't pay."

"So how would Newton know he was going to use his wife's van that day?"

"That I don't know."

"And does your squad think Newton was big enough to have Pearson killed, if he had a reason?"

"You don't have to be very big for that. Just have ten thousand dollars."

"So Pearson was keeping company with killers, but they picked a strange way to do him in, and they must have had information about the van."

Ranovic nodded. "It's pretty far out. Besides, if it was Newton, he would rather have his money. He might have arranged a little accident, a leg, maybe, as a warning."

"Okay. There's something else to be followed up, just to draw a line under it. Three people knew that Pearson was going to use that van—his wife and two guys named Leese and Nystrom. I don't think they are involved—where would they get hold of dynamite?"

"The same place anyone would. One of the gangs. It isn't hard."

"Okay. I'm going to make up a portfolio, those three and the five street traders. We've had a photographer working and we've got pictures of all of them. I'd like you to take the pictures over to your squad, and to the organized crime people, and see if any of them have been seen in the wrong places. I just want to eliminate the chance. Try any informers you know, and maybe the Don Jail, too."

"You aren't really hoping for anything, are you? I could walk my ass off going around asking people if they've ever seen any of them. I've got a better idea, just to demonstrate that you've checked them out. Why don't I go through the art gallery, the one the squad keeps, I mean."

"These people aren't on file."

Ranovic smiled. "One way or another, we've got pictures of everyone who goes near the people we're watching. That's what we do, take pictures, and compare them. We've got thousands of them. But I can still go through the lot in two or three hours. If I find anything, *then* I'll know who to ask if they've seen them. Okay, sir?''

Salter agreed. ''Pearson was still probably only giving the stuff away to get work. I wonder if he did line up girls?''

''He wasn't making enough for that, was he? They cost a hell of a lot of money. The whole hooker thing is wide open, anyway, now that they advertise in the Yellow Pages.''

''Probably. Okay, when you're satisfied either way, I think maybe it's time to drop your cover and see what you can find out as a cop. Brennan's done what he can, but you can do it again.''

Ranovic looked startled. ''Put a uniform on?''

''That isn't necessary. You don't want to surprise your old pals too much. Have you got a jacket and tie? Good. So go around the village, especially to the places near that garage and ask questions. See if anyone can remember anything. Who did they see around the garage that morning, or after the Princess went by? I know—thousands of people, but there's a chance they saw something odd. I don't know. Go over the ground with the garage attendants. Find me someone who saw something.''

Ranovic left and Salter returned to the letters. The first set were typed on cheap white paper and mailed in nonmatching envelopes, so that there was an awkward quarter inch folded over. Each letter contained the same message, ''Stop complaining about us or we will make you sorry,'' and signed, ''The Street Traders of Yorkville.''

The second set were typed on a different machine, according to the laboratory, on better-quality paper and mailed in matching envelopes.

The report attached to the letters was skimpy, and the only source of speculation lay in the difference between the two kinds of stationery, and the differences in the two mailing lists.

Salter began by confirming how the letters were delivered. "The first one was here when I came in that morning," the jeweler said. "Not mailed. You know, delivered by hand. The second one was mailed."

Everyone else told the same story.

None of the stores opened until ten o'clock, which allowed for plenty of time for the first batch to be delivered before they opened. No one could say who might have delivered them. Each day brought several deliveries of junk mail, and someone going from store to store with a bunch of envelopes would hardly be noticed.

Now, when Salter made the rounds of the stores, his reception was very different. The bomb had made the jeweler and the owner of the luggage store violent and somewhat justified in their demands for protection from the street traders. "Why can't you arrest those bastards?" the jeweler wanted to know as soon as Salter appeared. He pointed vaguely out to the empty street. "How many of us will have to get killed before you do anything?"

Asking questions of him and the luggage shop owner was useless. The Italian tailor was still puzzled as to why the first threat had included him. He was surprisingly indifferent to the street traders, or the threats. "They are just threats," he said. He also pointed out that maybe the bomb and the threats had nothing to do with each other. "Nobody says bomb in the letter, do they?" he said.

Vera wanted nothing to do with Salter. In answer to his questions, she said she had seen no one deliver the letters. When he asked her again about the street traders, in particular if any one peddler had abused her, she shook her head vehemently. "Not at all," she insisted. "No one has bothered me at all, no one."

Salter realized that the bomb terrified her, and she wanted no further part of being identified with the complaints. He gave up on her for the moment and returned to Lilliput, where he found Tommy Nystrom minding the bookstore. He felt a small sense of release as he walked into the store, as though he had come in out of the storm for a few moments, and he reminded himself that he was here to regard these people as suspects. Nevertheless, he accepted an offer of coffee from Nystrom, who had to go next door to buy it while Salter guarded the cash drawer. He took a chair beside the desk, and when Nystrom returned the two men settled in. "Do you know enough about these letters to answer some questions?" he began.

"Try me."

"Has Mrs. Pearson any idea who delivered them?"

"No. The first one just appeared. The second one came in the mail."

"She never got the first one, did she?"

"How do you mean?"

"There were two sets of letters. The message was similar, but there were lots of other differences. For one thing, the two sets didn't go to the same people."

"That's right, I forgot. But maybe Ruth got the first one and it got lost. Slipped under the mat like Tess's confession. I don't know." Nystrom shrugged, giving up on a not-very-interesting problem.

"The real question about the bookstore is why Mrs. Pearson got a letter at all. She never had a run-in with the traders, did she?"

"She can't remember offending any of them, and I'd be surprised if she did. It's not her style, she hates arguments. She always walks away from them."

They were interrupted by a child who wanted a book on dinosaurs, which Nystrom found for him.

"You know the stock pretty well," Salter said when Nystrom had handed the child his change.

"I spend a lot of time here. Without Ruth I'd be a little lost waif."

It was an odd description for a balding forty-year-old who was slightly fatter than he should be, but Salter let it pass. He finished his coffee and left the store, promising to let Nystrom know what their final decision about the house was, because if they decided to sell, Nystrom would welcome the listing. "I get the odd client looking for something north of St. Clair," he said.

"THEY SMELL NICE," Ranovic said. "What does the lab say about that?"

Salter sniffed the bunch of letters and reread the lab report. "The first batch are perfumed and they have identified it as Joy. The other batch doesn't smell. What do you make of that?"

"Let's see." Ranovic made a game of putting his hands behind his back and walking thoughtfully up and down the office. "Got it," he said. "The two sets of letters were sent by the same person, but he or she sent one set from work and one from home. She, I would think. Or, the two sets were sent by two different people."

"That's what I think."

"Which? Which 'that' do you think?"

"Both. I think they are the two possibilities. Now I'm going home." He picked up the letters and put the two bundles into separate pockets. "Call me tomorrow before you start out."

Before he went home Salter put a call in to Harry Wycke, the one colleague in Homicide he was on friendly terms with. He wanted to test what the reaction would be if he handed over the case in this state. Wycke was in his office and agreed to meet him for a beer in a pub on Jarvis Street. The entire force was still suffering from overwork, and Salter expressed his gratitude that Wycke was sparing him the time.

"Don't thank me, Charlie. If you don't clean this up, it will probably land on my desk next."

When Salter arrived at the pub, Wycke was already seated at one of the tables, tasting his beer suspiciously. "This is gourmet beer," he said. "Organically brewed with none of the proper chemicals. This batch is still fermenting. Get me a Molson's to wash it down, will you?"

Salter ordered the beer and told Wycke his story. Wycke stopped him before he had gone very far. "Did you check if the wife and her boyfriend came straight to the garage that morning?" he asked. "Did they pass a dynamite store on the way?"

"They didn't do it." Salter tried to sound dismissive.

"So you say. But, Christ, you haven't eliminated them yet, have you? I mean you've just *eliminated* them. Them and the gay deceiver, right?"

"I know they didn't do it."

"You don't know shit. You think they didn't because you like them. That's as bad as going after a guy because you don't like him and finding the evidence to fit. You're involved with these people, which is no way to run a homicide case. You know about the 24/24 rule?"

"I know about the 24/24 rule."

Wycke continued as if Salter had not spoken. "It means that the last twenty-four hours before a homicide and the twenty-four hours after are the most important."

Salter made an impatient gesture, but Wycke rolled on. "If you want to eliminate your pals find out what they were doing every minute in the twenty-four hours before the bomb. Where did they go? Who came to the house? And the same for Pearson's girlfriend. Check up on them all. You can't do much now about the other twenty-four hours. Never mind the chance he got killed instead of his wife. That would be a hit man, and Orliff's right. You won't find him. But don't pass it on to me until you've checked these people out because if you don't, I'll have to when the whole thing is stone cold. And that goes for the traders, too."

"They're clean, Harry. None of them have a record, not the bookstore people, nor any of the traders. I've checked them all out."

"I should fucking well hope so. Christ! But that's not what we're talking about. We're talking about the 24/24 rule as it applies to these people including those five street traders at least. We're talking about the mess I will inherit when the whole fucking thing is stone goddamn cold."

Salter swallowed his beer in silence.

"Orliff's probably right, anyway," Wycke said, relenting a little. "When your chief suspect is dead, you've got problems. You're probably wasting your time."

Salter had got what he came for, an unreassuring outside comment on his handling of the case, and Wycke had killed any further discussion. Salter switched the subject to Wycke's fishing cottage, which allowed them to finish their beer and leave.

BUT DRIVING HOME, turning over the implications of the 24/24 rule in his mind, he grabbed at something else he had not done which might pile the burden of circumstantial evidence so high that even Wycke would accept it.

"Smell these," Salter said when he got home.

Annie picked up the bundle of letters, inhaled, and said, "Who are they from? Your girlfriend?"

"The laboratory said it's Joy."

"So it is. I made you buy me some at the airport when we came back from England."

"I need your nose. Have you got an hour tomorrow morning?"

"Sure. Make it late and I'll take my lunch hour. What do I have to do?"

Salter explained. He was notorious around his own house for being unable to see or smell like a normal human being. He never looked at pictures, or scenery, and had no visual memory at all. As for smell, when Annie walked into the house, sniffing and saying, "What's that?" his reaction was always irritation because the smell of burning, or escaping gas or new-mown hay or whatever else had struck her nostrils on the doorstep had escaped him utterly. Now he wanted to test her out. "It's an idea I've had. One of the peddlers suggested it."

So the next day at noon Annie duly went from store to store in Yorkville, paying particular attention to the list Salter had given her, wandering into the back rooms by mistake, bumping into the owners as she turned suddenly. When she had completed her rounds she met Salter for a bowl of goulash at the Coffee Mill.

"It's Vera," she said, when they had given their order.

"I thought it might be. I should have listened harder to those street traders. Are you sure?"

"I'm sure Vera is drenched in Joy. I checked the perfume counter of Holt, Renfrew before I started. She's it, all right."

"I can't pinch her for wearing perfume, though. I'll have to confirm it somehow. Thanks."

"That was fun. You don't get much Sherlock-type stuff, do you?"

"No, thank Christ, or I'd have to take you around with me."

"Aren't you going to tell me what it's all about?"

"He never tells Watson, does he?"

"Who?"

"Watson. The dummy. I'll tell you tonight."

"This little consultation is going to cost you two hundred dollars. Vera is very good at selling."

Salter looked around her chair for a parcel. "Where is it?"

"I didn't have the cash and I realized that I'd better not use the charge card in case she recognized your name. The same with our checks."

"You silly cow," Salter said. "What did you do, then?"

"I left a deposit. I'll pick it up tomorrow. When you've given me the money. Now I have to go. Enough cops and robbers. I've got work to do."

Salter deposited her at her Church Street studio, and returned to his office. It took him the rest of the afternoon to get a sample from Vera's typewriter; eventually he tracked one down at City Hall, where the Works Department had several letters from her on file, complaining about the sidewalk. The experts at the laboratory compared this sample with the letters and confirmed that the first batch had indeed emanated from Vera, but just as certainly the second set of letters hadn't, differing from the first as much in typescript as they did in smell.

"Why?" Orliff asked. "What was she up to?"

"I'll find out in the morning."

"Making mischief?"

"Ask me tomorrow," Salter said.

FOURTEEN

THE NEXT MORNING Salter was Vera's first customer. Bracing himself for a noisy session, he produced a copy of the complaints she had written to City Hall. "Did you write this letter, ma'am?" he asked mildly. Her signature was on the bottom.

Her reaction was totally in keeping with his sense that lately she had become more afraid than hostile. "I don't know. I wrote something like that, sure, to the city when the sidewalks were so bad. They still are. Why?"

Salter resisted the slightly sadistic impulse to force her to agree that this particular letter was the one she had written. "May I see the machine—your typewriter, please?"

She collapsed immediately. "What do you want to see it for? Sure it's mine. I wrote the letter, sure. So what do you want?"

"Does anyone else use the typewriter?"

She screwed her face up at the question, looking for an escape for herself in it. Then she shook her head and waited for the next question. Salter produced the bundle of threatening letters and she promptly sat on a chair and started to howl, drumming her feet on the floor and covering her face with her hands. Salter locked the door of the store, turned the sign to CLOSED, and returned to Vera, waiting. Soon her howls declined to paroxysms of sniffing and then to silence as she waited with her head down for Salter's next move.

"There'll be charges, of course," he said. "Public mischief, I think, but I'm not concerned with that right now. What were you trying to do?" He didn't believe for a second that Vera had had anything to do with bombs.

"I was trying to get rid of those sodding traders," she shouted, her accent becoming stronger with her returning anger. "I have worked hard all my bloody life since I left school, everything is in this business, and now some scum comes along to ruin me. The police don't care, the city doesn't care, nobody cares except my customers, who won't come here if the streets are full of beggars and touts. So, yes, I sent those letters to make you listen, just those, not the second ones. Somebody else saw my idea and—oh, it's terrible." She started to howl again.

Salter was slightly embarrassed by her extravagant emotional display, but not moved. When she was once more quiet, he asked, "You have no idea who sent the second letters?"

"How could I? When I got it, I thought someone was using my idea to make a joke, just to frighten people, you know. That wasn't my idea. I wanted to make the police keep the street traders out of Yorkville. And then this bomb." She looked at Salter in a distraught fashion. "It must be a madman."

"I doubt it," Salter said. He watched her subside. "Are you all right, now?" Are you going to open the store?"

"How can I open the store now?" she cried. "With everyone knowing."

"No one knows yet, except me. I've got to lay charges, but it'll take some time."

She began to gather herself together. "When?" she asked. "When will they know?"

"I can't tell you. It could be months before the case comes up. Until then all anyone will know is that you've been charged with some kind of mischief. If the papers don't get hold of it you might be okay until the court trial. Get a lawyer.''

''Sure,'' she said, thinking now. ''I'll get a lawyer. And a partner to run the store for a while. That's it.'' She got up and looked in a mirror. ''God, what a mess.'' She turned around to face Salter. ''Is there anything I have to say now? I admit I wrote the letters. There's the type-writer. What happens next?''

''Just type a few words for me on a piece of paper. Sign your name. I'll arrange for you to be charged. I won't arrest you in front of the customers.''

''I'll be grateful for that.'' She did as she was told. ''Now let me fix my face.''

Salter left her at the mirror and walked through to Yorkville to where his car was parked on Hazelton Avenue. Vera's bit of mischief had suggested a line on the second batch of letters, and he wanted to think through his next move.

There was a rapping at the car window. A parking official stood in the road, his notebook poised. Salter shook his head, mouthed ''No thanks,'' and drove off.

IN THE OFFICE he laid out the problem to Constable Brennan, after congratulating him on his efficient questioning. ''First, find out from City Hall who the tenants are on Cumberland and Yorkville. Find out who the landlords are, too. Who owns the building, if the storekeeper doesn't. Then I want an example of the typing from every source. I don't know, they probably write some kind of letter when they pay their taxes, or retail licenses or whatever. Somebody at City Hall will know. Then, when you've got a sample of typing from every store, and every landlord, take them down to the lab and have them compare them with this." He held out one of the second batch of letters. "I want to know if any of them wrote these letters. See?"

The constable nodded, but he looked worried, like a conscientious child being sent on a difficult errand, knowing there would be problems when he got to the store. "I'll be here," Salter said, recognizing the signs. "Call me if you get bogged down." At that the policeman went off cheerfully enough and Salter settled in to distract himself by working on the final report on picket violence.

LATER, SALTER TOLD Annie about his success with Vera. They were sitting in the backyard on one of the longest, warmest nights of the year.

"What about the second lot of letters?" she asked.

"I'm hoping for the same kind of luck with those. If not, I don't know. But even if I'm lucky and find out who sent them, it may not be any help, except to eliminate some possibilities. It may be another Vera."

"We go to the Island in ten days. I hope your case is cleared up by then."

"They'll take it away from me soon. Now that the Princess has gone, they'll bring in the experts. Made up your mind about the house yet?"

"Yes, I think your friend gave me the answer."

"Nystrom?"

"Yes. Putting the kitchen in the front is a great idea. I want to start work on it when we come back from the Island."

"Did you ever have any gay friends?" Salter asked her suddenly.

"Men?"

"Yeah. Like Nystrom."

"I've been married to you for twenty years. Before that I worked in Dad's hotel on the Island. There weren't any gays in the Maritimes in the sixties, except the skating coach. Why?"

"I was just wondering."

"What?"

"About Nystrom and Ruth Pearson."

"Diane Ferguson has a friend like that. They call each other every day and eat lunch or dinner at least twice a week."

"She's married?"

"Oh, sure. Very much so."

"What's the attraction?"

"I would guess it's about the most uncomplicated relationship you can have, once you both relax. I get the sense from Diane that the two of them are very intimate without, you know, being intimate."

"But isn't that what *women* friends are for?"

Annie considered this. "The other would be more loyal. They'd trust each other more."

"You think so?"

Now Annie gained some assurance as she reflected. "Yes. I've never heard Diane say a word about any shortcomings her friend has. He's not like the rest of her life, to be gossiped about and maybe judged, not even a little."

"Like some kind of ideal brother/sister thing?"

Annie shook her head. "Not like anything I can think of."

They stopped talking as a raccoon came toward them from the end of the yard. As they watched, it reached the edge of the deck and began to haul itself up. This brought it within a few feet of them, and Salter cleared his throat to warn it off. True to its burglar mask, it waddled off into a neighbor's yard, searching for some unguarded garbage.

"Who's 'we' these days?" Salter asked.

"What?"

"Who's 'we'? You said 'we' are going to the Island. Is Angus coming?"

"He hasn't spoken to me since he said he wasn't, so I guess he isn't."

"You are going to let him stay here with her?"

"How could I stop him? He can cook for himself better than you can. He can run the washing machine. What else is there that might prevent him?"

"Her mother?"

"I phoned her today and told her exactly what our plans were for July, so she could worry about Angela if she had a mind. She seemed puzzled—I don't really know her—as if she was trying to figure out why I was telling her all this. So I have done my duty. The hell with it."

"And that's it? We just leave them to it?"

"Unless you feel like imposing martial law. I don't. What's the problem, Charlie? You against premarital sex? Or against knowing about it? Or against it in your house? Or are they too young? How old would be okay? Speak, Charlie, speak. Tell me what the problem is." She looked at his face. "Or is something wrong at work?"

"The problem is that when I was his age and older, getting laid in Toronto, even in Cabbagetown, was very, very hard and much appreciated when it happened. Four of us saved up once and went down to Buffalo, but when we got there we chickened out. That's the way it was when I was seventeen. I think these kids have it too easy." Salter began to warm to his subject. "They don't get any proper initiation. Sex, for a single lad from a nice home, ought to be forbidden, yearned after, rare, dangerous, totally unsatisfactory the first few times, and a terrific accomplishment. If not, the whole institution crumbles."

"What—marriage?"

"No." Salter thought. He was talking about something real, he knew that. What? "Puberty, I think. Maybe marriage, too."

She laughed. "You're jealous, Salter. But think of it this way. You can be sure, one way or another, that they are going to have just as many problems as we did. You, I mean. I didn't have any problems."

"You would've if I hadn't come along and solved them."

A voice came through the darkness from the neighbor's patio. "Could you speak up please, Charlie? We're dying to hear how you did it."

They moved inside the house. "Didn't Dad phone?" Salter asked. "Is Seth leaving him alone?"

"Oh, yes. I forgot. He asked how much the tapes that Seth is using cost, and where he could buy some."

"Some? How long does he plan to talk?"

"Seth goes over there every day after school. Today I think he talked for an hour."

"Where are they up to?"

"Seth said that today he was talking about the newspaper route he had when he was eleven, but it's not strictly chronological."

"This could go on for months, or miles if it's tape we're talking about."

"It's all right, though, isn't it?"

"Oh, sure. How many tapes has Seth got?"

"Three already."

"When does he play them back, edit them, or whatever they do?"

"I don't know if he's gotten to that point. Right now he's making little labels, 'Grandfather's History: Volume 1.' He's cleared a space on his bookshelves." There was a long pause. "*Is* there something wrong?"

"Nah, not really "

"With Seth?"

"No, no."

"Angus?"

"No, what the hell. *He* can't get pregnant."

"Me? Us?"

He leaned over and put a hand on her neck.

"What then?" she persisted. "Something's the matter."

"Not around here. Like you said. Work."

"Orliff, or the bombing case?"

"The case. It may be insoluble. I'm certain that none of the three in the bookshop, nor any of the traders, had anything to do with it, but unless I find out who did, Homicide will start all over again and I'm not going to look very good."

"How long have you got?"

"A few days, if that."

"What about the new man? Any word?"

"What? Oh, no. Nothing. I'm not too concerned about that anymore." He waited for her to ask why. When she said nothing, he continued. "I've decided to quit," he announced.

Annie said nothing.

"Not because of Cresswell, or anyone else. I just feel too old to break in a new boss."

Still Annie said nothing.

"I've been lucky with Orliff. But I don't want to transfer, and I'm not going to be lucky a second time. The new guy will probably be younger than I am—probably want me to take a computer course or some damn thing. Besides, he should have the chance to find his own men. I don't think Gatenby will stay around long, either.'' Aren't you even going to give me an argument, he wondered. "Make you happy?" he asked.

"What will you do? You're too young to sit on the porch all day."

"And too old to start in at something else?"

Annie shook her head, brushing the notion aside. "What does this case matter, then?"

"I'd like to leave clean. If I screw this up, that's the one they'll remember. I want to go out a winner."

"When did you feel like resigning?"

"When Orliff told me he was going. We talked about it, remember?"

"That's when the idea came up, but you were just testing the waters. But this is different. Now you sound resigned to it—resigned to resigning, I mean. It's partly this case, isn't it?"

Salter waited for her to continue, allowing her, as he had done so often in the past, to clarify his internal world.

"What it sounds like to me is that you're getting ready, if you don't solve this case, to pretend it doesn't matter, because you were planning to quit, anyway. But the other side of you says it does matter because you want to go out while you're on top. You're in a muddle, Charlie. I'd forget about resigning until the case is over. Then you can think about the future. Resigning's got nothing to do with this case. Solving it, or not, is what matters. Pretend you're ten years younger and just concentrate on the job."

"Orliff thinks it matters. To me, I mean."

"Orliff wants to hand you over as a going concern. Forget about Orliff. He's always figuring the angles. The case has nothing to do with whether you resign. It would be nice to go out on top but that's not the best reason for trying to find a killer, is it?''

Salter digested the implications of this. ''It's not just this case. I *have* been thinking about resigning a lot, and it doesn't feel bad.''

''Good. So after the case is finished, and after you find out what the new man is like, you can think about it some more. Then, if you're sure the salt has lost its savor, quit.''

''And then?''

''Oh, Jesus, I don't know. Let's talk about it then.''

In bed, he said, ''There's just one problem.'' He caressed the base of her spine. ''My old man.''

''Your father?''

''Yeah. If I quit, or rather, whenever I quit, anytime before I'm sixty-five, he'll tell me I never finish anything. He's been waiting twenty-five years for me to quit so that he can be right again. He thinks you should only have one job in your life.''

Annie laughed. ''Maybe the time has come for a confrontation. Now take your hand away and let's get some sleep.''

FIFTEEN

CONSTABLE BRENNAN reported in the next morning on his way to City Hall. "I'm not getting ahead very fast. It's a big job. I could be on it for weeks."

"It's like that sometimes. Maybe you'll get lucky early," Salter told him, unsympathetically. He was more concerned with himself than he was with Brennan's misery, as he tried to make sure he had done all he should. As he brooded, he remembered that he had not done anything more about the Stoney Lake forger since he got back, and he turned to the case now, relieved at being able to postpone thinking about bombs even for a few minutes. He dug out the list of cottage owners he had checked off at the marina and began calling them to ask if any of them had rented their cottages recently. He was trusting Hector that none of the owners had ever been seen painting.

He got as far as the fourth name before he was interrupted by a call from Mrs. Beldin. "You've got all our phones humming," she said. "We're all wondering what's going on. I know, of course. I should have thought of it myself and put you on the right track immediately. Right under my nose. The people you are looking for are the Carstairs. They haven't used their cottage for three years. They rent it to a man named Ockenden—that's all we know about him. He lives secretly there, with a guard dog. He's your man. We've all tried to find out about him but he won't accept any invitations for drinks, he doesn't go to church, and if you go near the cottage he comes down on the dock to repel boarders. He's your man, all right. How stupid of me.''

"Easy, Mrs. Beldin. Easy. He may just be a hermit. Which is the Carstairs cottage?''

"Green and white, with a weather vane. Hector will point it out. Do let me know what you find out, won't you. First, I mean. I could make it a little item for the papers and have them mention my book.''

"You'll be the first.''

Next he phoned the Carstairs' number and got an answering machine. No sooner had he hung up than Mrs. Beldin rang again. "I forgot to tell you. The Carstairs are in Russia or somewhere, so you won't get an answer from them. Better go straight up to the lake.'' Mrs. Beldin was used to giving orders.

"Thanks for calling,'' Salter said.

He had made the calls as a distraction, to allow his larger problems to cook a little, and now he tried to return, mentally, to Yorkville. But the appearance of Ockenden was an even larger distraction, and a trip to the lake would take the rest of the day and give him a chance to think some more, he told himself.

What began in self-justification ended in truth. On the drive up to the lake, he could think of nothing else but the Yorkville case, and by the time he arrived he had achieved a further clarification for himself. What stuck out for him now was that Vera had sent a letter to herself to divert suspicion away from herself, and the bookstore had received only the second letter. Thus he came in his thinking to the possibility that he might be absolutely wrong in his assumption that any or all of the bookstore trio were innocent, and that he had better get a sample from the store's typewriter. Vera had just been making mischief, but if the second batch of letters came from the bookstore it was worse than mischief and he needed to find that out quickly. And if, as he firmly believed, there was no connection between the second batch of letters and the bookstore, then his investigation was probably over, unless Brennan got lucky.

As he approached the Carstairs cottage, three hours later, he saw a man leave the building and disappear into a smaller cabin at the edge of the lake. A large Alsatian dog padded down to meet Salter as he touched the dock. He looked at Salter thoughtfully, not making a sound, and Salter cupped his hands around his mouth and shouted, "Anybody home?" ready to back off at the first sign from the dog.

After that it was easy. Ockenden came out of the cabin and Salter begged a drink of water from him.

"I wondered when you would come by," Ockenden said.

"You wondered?"

"I saw you fooling about on the lake a few days ago. Didn't catch much, did you?"

"Couple of pickerel." Salter became aware that Ockenden was playing a game.

Ockenden nodded. "I got careless and you got lucky. Someone finally put two and two together. You might say I've been waiting for you ever since that story came out. All right, come on up." He said a word to the dog, who smiled and sniffed Salter's hand as the inspector tied up the boat at the dock.

The painter led the way inside the small cabin and pointed through the window. "There it is," he said. "It" was the view in the forged painting, perfectly framed by the window.

Salter produced his identification, but Ockenden waved it away. "I painted the picture," he said. "And these, too.'' he showed Salter half a dozen others, all freshly painted landscapes of the kind familiar to every Canadian schoolchild. "I got careless," Ockenden said again. "Usually I go somewhere else to find a scene, but I was busy with my own work and I dashed that one off without thinking. I knew Amis Settle lived here once."

"How many have you painted?"

"Ten or fifteen. I don't know."

"You don't sign them?"

"No. That's how they leave me." He pointed to the little stack of paintings. "I have no idea what happens next. I've been told they turn up at London auctions, looking a bit older. Someone buys them off my agent, that's all I know. I'm surprised that it hasn't been done before. They are childishly easy to imitate, forge, if that's what you want to call it. Shit, that's what they are. Absolute shit. I can do one in an afternoon. Four trees, three rocks, a cloud, and a bit of lake. Painting by numbers. Now these, on the other hand, are masterpieces and I can't sell one of them. These are the ones I wanted you to see."

The painter led Salter to a row of pictures that hung on the back wall of the cabin. Each one was marked by, to Salter, a strikingly original technique. In each case, a perfectly ordinary scene contained an optical magnification of some aspect of itself that lay beneath the surface. A picture of a lake focused on a small area in which the lake surface had been replaced by a tiny painting of a trout. The trout was thus hundreds of times larger than the scale of the painting, although only taking up half-an-inch of canvas. The lake had been opened up like an Advent calendar to reveal the fish beneath the surface. The illusion was further enhanced by a series of whorls around the fish, so that the final effect was as if a bull's-eye lens had been placed over the spot on the lake, magnifying it and dragging the fish up to the eye.

Another picture was of a room in which a man was writing at a desk. In this one the magnified spot was inside the man's head where a small metal canister was embedded in one lobe of the brain. Another was a scene of some woods on the other side of a lake. Deep within the trees was an owl, tearing the head off a mouse. Yet another was a cocktail party that focused on the back of a young girl where the artist had chosen to reveal, beneath the dress, a safety pin holding together the straps of her brassière. There were a dozen pictures along the wall; the tone varied from ordinary magic (the fish), to comic (the safety pin), to the horrible (the owl). Two of them were obscene. Salter found the idea of the pictures riveting.

"You see what I'm driving at?" the artist inquired eagerly.

"No."

"It's a matter of vision. Do you know what cubism is?"

"Of course," Salter said. Two eyes on one side of a head.

"The cubists showed us that realism is only one form of reality. I am doing the same."

"I see."

"What do you see?"

Salter had two rules when confronted with aesthetic problems. The first was never, under any circumstances, to pretend to admit to an understanding of the incomprehensible. The second was to assume that it was all bullshit. He wondered whether to add a third: Assume the artist is insane, a victim of a private delusion. "It's science fiction," he said, forgetting all his rules as he realized with excitement what was going on in the pictures. "If you could see something three miles away and bring it close up, and if you had X-ray vision to start with, this is what you would be able to see." And then he realized what in fact it was. "It's like bugging the world visually," he said. "We've got microphones now that will let us hear what those two guys across the lake are saying to each other." Salter pointed through the window to two dots seated in a canoe on the other side of the lake. "What you've done is to use a kind of visual mike that can pick up anything at any distance, right? Be terrific if we had one." Salter felt as he had once felt in grade eleven when, a mediocre math student, he had once, gloriously, been the only student who could see how to solve a particular geometry problem.

"Is that what you think?" The artist's voice was quiet, tentative, his demeanor sour. Salter realized that he had in some way understood too much and thereby lowered the status of the artist's vision, demonstrated the cliché behind the magic.

"They're terrific," he said. "But if I can read them you're going to get a lot of imitators."

"Am I? Am I indeed? We'll see. But what are you going to do about my other imitations?"

"I'll check with your agent. If what you say is true, then maybe it's someone else's problem."

And so it proved. Salter returned to Toronto in time to call on the agent, though not before the agent had been warned by Ockenden that he was coming. But the agent was not worried. He had all the proof to show that he shipped the pictures to a dealer in Switzerland, "for what they were worth." He had heard, he said, that from Switzerland the pictures went to Upper Slaughter and then to London. He had not realized that someone aged them along the way, and he intended to write to the London gallery immediately and let them know how appalled he was.

The problem was one for the English, if anybody, and Salter left the gallery to think about a report to be distributed to Canadian dealers and art galleries.

THE NEXT MORNING he set out to call on the bookstore. As he walked down Cumberland, Tommy Nystrom appeared from the Cakemaster and opened up the bookstore, which he had apparently closed while he got himself some coffee.

Salter gave him another ten minutes, wondering how he was going to get what he wanted—simply asking for a sample from the machine would not be smart at this stage—when a couple appeared, dressed in brightly colored trousers, hung about with photographing machines and surrounded by children. They paused outside the bookstore, wondering whether to make a video of walking down the steps, then, at the insistence of the children, pressed into the store without recording it. When this family was followed by another with three children, Salter decided he had what he wanted and crossed the street to the store.

Inside, Nystrom was standing behind the cash register, watching, as the children darted excitedly from book to book, and the two pairs of adults struck up an acquaintance in the center of the store, comparing their experiences with children and books.

"More questions, Inspector?" Nystrom asked, his eyes on the children. "Or has your wife gotten another idea about the house?"

"I was really looking for Mrs. Pearson," Salter said. "She still at home?"

"She'll be in a bit later. She's okay, really, and she's got to face the vulgar mob sometime. I can only give her a couple of hours this afternoon. David's coming down then, I think."

"I'll go over to the house and see her there. Would you call her and tell her to expect me?" Then, as Nystrom moved to the phone, he said, "Maybe you can help me, save me a call. I just want to get everyone's movements straight. As far as you know, Mrs. Pearson came in at what, eight-thirty on Saturday? She parked in the garage, then never returned to the van all day, right? But she did leave the store to see the Princess?"

"Right. The garage was closed off at nine, you know. No one could get in after that."

Salter nodded. "David Leese came into the store at twelve and stayed until six. That right?"

"Yes."

"You *saw* him, or is that what you were told?"

"I saw him. I was here all day on Saturday, I told you."

"By yourself?"

"No, Lotta, the part-time girl was here. She only works afternoons. But it was crowded, though no one was buying much, so we all four stayed all afternoon to clear the crowd." Nystrom broke off to accept the money from one of the children. The first passion of the children to see everything in the store had nearly spent itself and the two families were beginning to regroup to continue on their way. Two more children were waiting to buy books. Salter decided he would not get a better opportunity, and he leaned close to Nystrom's ear. "Can I use the washroom?" he asked. "Do you have one?"

"In the back. Through the door, then around to the left. Over in the far corner."

Salter let himself in through the door at the back of the store and found himself in the area he remembered. A Smith-Corona portable electric typewriter sat on the corner of the desk. Salter glanced around for a piece of correspondence or a bill he could steal, but everything seemed to be filed away. Then, beside the chair he saw a wastebasket with a crumpled draft of a letter resting on top of the other rubbish. He walked over to the door in the corner, which opened onto a tiny washroom, just big enough for the toilet and washbasin it held, and flushed the toilet. Taking his time, with his back to the door leading to the store, he fished out the crumpled letter from the basket and smoothed it out on the desk. When he was sure he had what he wanted, he folded the letter and stuffed it into his wallet. He emerged into the store to find it empty and Nystrom tidying the shelves.

"Crowded in there," he said.

"Did we finish the questions?"

"Not quite. I'd like to double-check also who knew where everyone was on the day Pearson was killed. He called his wife, didn't he? On Friday night. Said he was going to need the van?"

"That's what Ruth said."

"When? When did she say that?"

"On Saturday."

"When did she tell Leese?"

"On Friday, I would think. They live together, you know. No more about other people, please. Ask *them*."

"I'll ask who I like, but I'm just double-checking."

"You still want me to tell Ruth you're coming?" Nystrom picked up the phone.

"No, I'll catch her another time."

"I *will* tell her you were asking after her, though."

I bet you will, Salter thought. "Sure," he said. "I just want to know who knew Pearson was going to use the van." Salter put out his hand, a rare gesture with him, but a usefully disconcerting one sometimes. Nystrom looked surprised, then shook hands somewhat embarrassedly.

RANOVIC WAS SITTING on a bench across the street, looking self-conscious in a newish-looking suit and tie, as though he were dressed to apply for a job. He had been questioning the garage attendants for the third or fourth time to see if they remembered anything.

"Any luck?" Salter asked.

"Nothing. I've been over the area three times."

"So go over it again. Somewhere around here someone saw something. So keep asking."

"Sir, they're seeing me coming! Old 'where-were-you-on-Saturday-afternoon,' they're calling me."

"Sticks and stones, Gorgi."

"Huh?"

"Sticks and stones will break my bones but names can't hurt me."

"What's that? An old Indian proverb?"

"No, English. Don't they have one like it in Yugoslavia?"

"Yeah, it goes..." Ranovic uttered a few words of Croatian.

"What does it mean?"

"If you pay my wages, you can insult me, too."

Salter returned to his office and arranged for the letter he had stolen to be delivered to the laboratory and compared with the second set of letters. He waited for a reply and it came within the hour. The letter had not been typed on the Lilliput machine, which was a very new model, but on something rather older, although of the same make.

Thank Christ! he thought. That's it, then. He went home.

THE NEXT MORNING he got an anonymous phone call.

"You in charge of de bombin'?" the voice asked. It sounded like the voice of every small-time thug that Salter had ever seen on television.

"Who are you?"

"De name's Brasker. You in charge of de bombin'?"

"What do you want?"

"I wanna make a patch."

"You want to what?"

"I wanna make a patch, give you some information. I heard dese two guys talkin' about a contract on someone."

"Where?"

"In a bar. What's the difference?"

"When?"

"Jesus Christ. About three weeks ago. What's the difference?"

"Why were they talking with you around?"

"They thought I was passed out, see." There was a pause. "But I wasn't, I was on Demerol so I looked kinda out of it. But I was okay and one of these guys started talking about how he was going to lose some money if he went away. He'd got a contract, a real easy one, some guy who runs a bookstore."

"A contract to kill someone who runs a bookstore?"

"That's right. Blow him away, like."

"Any names?"

"Nah."

"Who put the contract out?"

"I didn't hear."

"And that's it? You heard a guy tell someone he had a contract to kill a bookstore owner?"

"That's it. You tryin' to trace this call?"

"Who were these guys?"

"One of them was Joe Dorval."

"Who's that?"

"A guy."

"So why are you telling me? You want some money?"

"Nah. Just get Dorval. De fucker screwed me up one time."

"Where can I find you if I want you?"

But Brasker had hung up.

SALTER ASKED FOR some time with Sergeant Crosbie, who ran the organized crime detail. In Crosbie's office he told him the story of the call. "What do you make of that?" he finished.

"It happens. Not often. Usually we pay for the real information. It can happen this way, but I'll tell you, it's probably someone with a grudge. Nothing to do with the bombing."

"You ever heard of these guys?"

"Nope. Brasker, you say, and Dorval?" Crosbie typed for a few minutes at a terminal in the corner of the room. "No Brasker," he said. "No record of one, so he was giving you a phony name. And the only Dorval is doing time in New Brunswick. His name's Louis, not Joe."

"So what's going on?"

"You're dealing with amateurs. You could try the homicide detail, see if they know them. It sounds a little phony."

"But it *could* be on the up-and-up."

"Sure. For a start, he wouldn't use his own name, would he? He just made that up. And maybe he knows the guy as

Joe Dorval but we know him as something else. So it could be a real conversation he overheard. I wish I'd heard him. I might have known the voice. I know a lot of these guys. I pay some of them."

Salter was out of his depth. "Can an ordinary citizen put out a contract? A murder contract?"

Crosbie reminded Salter of a recent celebrated case where an extraordinary but not otherwise criminal citizen had done just that.

"But he bungled it, didn't he? Or they did."

"That's right. Maybe that answers your question. An ordinary citizen would be able to, but he'd leave a trace a mile wide looking for someone to do it. He wouldn't know where to start, so, just to find a hit man he'd ask a lot of people. No pro would touch it; he'd have to find a hard case stupid enough to take his money and not just disappear with it. Because we would hear, like from one of our real stoolies or an undercover man, probably before he found someone."

"It *could* happen, though."

"Sure. What was the method? What did they use?"

"A car bomb. Triggered by a push button under the seat or the wheel."

Crosbie shook his head. "That's a pro, and they don't go around talking in front of guys like Brasker. Sorry."

ORLIFF HEARD HIM OUT, then pointed out the possibility. "The bomb is professional, but the bomber may not be, is that right? What we need to do is concentrate on the bomb. How would an amateur get hold of a bomb like that?"

"He'd have to make a connection."

"Maybe we can find that out. What about this guy, Sticky Newton? He's the obvious connection."

"Only if Pearson set the bomb. Not if it was someone else."

Orliff shook his head. "Newton could maybe find out if someone bought a bomb lately."

"He isn't going to do that. Why should he?"

"Because otherwise we will nail him with these bits and pieces they can get him on. Let's lean on Newton a bit, see if he'll trade."

But Orliff and Salter did not own Newton; Newton belonged to the organized crime detail. He belonged to Crosbie.

"No way," Crosbie said. "In the first place, I don't deal with these bastards. If we can't get the job done without getting into bed with a lot of murderers, then let's wait until we can. I don't hold with amnesty."

"Newton isn't a murderer, Joe. You said so yourself."

"He's part of it. The way he makes his living, people get murdered, even if he doesn't pull the trigger. I want to nail him."

"You haven't got much on him."

"I know that. That's why I'm holding off. I've got enough to stick him for six months, but I want him in Kingston for seven years."

"You'll get him eventually. But he could be what I need right now to wrap this thing up, remove suspicion from some harmless citizens."

"No. In the second place, if I give you Newton, that would be three months' work down the drain." Crosbie was getting angry. "What about those people in the bookstore? Why wouldn't one of those have paid to off Pearson?"

"They wouldn't know how."

"What about that fag? Maybe he's into rough trade. They know plenty of thugs, those people."

"Not this one." Salter watched Crosbie thrash around, grasping at straws, guessing that he was angry that he might have to give up Newton whether he liked it or not. He could not afford to alienate Crosbie, too. He said, "Newton's yours, Joe. If you want to keep him that's the end of it."

"Until Orliff asks my boss to order me to give him to you. Right?"

"No. That's the end of it. I'll try something else."

"You can't have him. Fuck it." Crosbie walked out of the office.

An hour later he phoned Salter. "Are you going up the line for Newton, or not?" he asked.

"I told you. No. He's yours."

"All right, you can have him. He's not worth a hell of a lot, anyway. It's not the way I work but if you want to operate that way it's no skin off my nose. But it's wrong. I'll tell you something though, Salter. If you had tried to get an order, you wouldn't have gotten one. I had a talk with my boss. He was all set to back me. Newton's mine, but you can have him."

"Thanks. Now, will you reel him in for me?"

"I'll talk to him. What do you want to know?"

Salter explained. When Crosbie called back it was to say that Newton was willing to cooperate. "Even the prospect of ninety days in the Don Jail scares the shit out of him. He's getting old. Worth more to us than I thought."

In the meantime, Salter interviewed Ruth Pearson, who was now back in the store. He had to cover the possibility that the phone call was genuine.

"We're certain now, on information received, that the bomb was intended for your husband," he said. "So I would like you to rack your brains and tell me who else could possibly have known that he would be using the truck that day."

She held steady in the face of the obvious implication, then started. "First of all, David. My husband telephoned for the van on Thursday, so I had plenty of time to tell David, especially as it would mean we would be without the van on Sunday. He doesn't have a car. Then Tommy. I'm sure I told him on Friday. Yes, I did, because he was going to give us all a ride home on Saturday. Either David or Tommy might have told other people, but I don't remember telling anyone else. Why should I have? But all three of us knew." She continued to look steadily at him.

The truth, the whole truth, and nothing but the truth, Salter thought. Look at her. She knows they aren't involved but if she's wrong she wants to know about it. Out of sympathy and some admiration for her, he said, "What we don't know, of course, is who your husband told, which is probably the answer to this whole thing."

"I think it is. It isn't going to be easy, is it?"

SIXTEEN

THE FIRST WORD from Newton was negative. There was no contract on Pearson. If that was true, they agreed, that was something, and Newton was sent down the hole again, protesting, to find out what he was asked in the first place: Had anyone been buying bombs lately?

The next day, Brasker called again. "I just remembered sump'n'," he said, in his Damon Runyonish voice. "Listen, I'll tell you quick before you can trace this call. Okay. I got it wrong. The contract was on a woman. I don't know her name. It was on a woman who runs a bookstore, that's what I heard. That's why they had trouble letting it. Some guys won't take a contract on a woman."

"Why did you say it was a guy?"

"I was nervous, talkin' to the fuzz. It was a woman, though. That's what I heard."

"That it?"

"Yeah. No. Sump'n' else. The contract's run out. There isn't any contract anymore." Brasker hung up.

SALTER, ORLIFF, AND CROSBIE considered the message. "I think he's feeding you bullshit," Crosbie said. "Contracts don't run out. They expire when the target is dead. The man gets paid up front and if he doesn't do his job or return the money, then there'll be a contract out on *him*. Contracts don't expire."

"You're talking about the mob."

"Who are *you* talking about? The Happy Gang?"

"Amateurs, like you said. The kind of people who let contracts expire."

"Like who?"

"Like Pearson."

"I still think it's bullshit," Crosbie said. "But good luck. Don't forget you owe me a very big favor one of these days." He left them to it.

"If you're right," Orliff said, "then this *is* the end of the line. They bombed the truck on the one day they knew he was using it. I'm sorry, Charlie. This is what I was afraid of. Maybe in five years' time someone will talk, but in the meantime you're stuck with a theory and an open case. Not very tidy, but there's nothing else to do."

"Maybe Newton will come up with something."

"I doubt it. I think we're finished."

Or I am, Salter thought, and began his report. He labored for some time and came to the second group of letters, and how he had confirmed that they were not from Lilliput. Then, setting the report aside, he made a brief summary of the subsequent events. Looking for the flaws that Orliff (or his successor) might see, he became consumed with the conviction that someone was trying to con him. He replayed the voice of Brasker in his head, hearing again the absurd stage-gangster accent, and he listened with all of Crosbie's skepticism. He took another piece of paper and started again to make a list, this time paying close attention to the timing of the events, trying to find a place and a reason for someone to insert a red herring into the investigation, because he was becoming certain that that was what was happening. He came to the scene where he was checking on the Lilliput typewriter, and then he knew, with no basis of proof whatsoever, who was interfering. He started to pick up the phone, and then stopped, seeing how carefully he would have to move. He began to write a new scenario, a dialogue designed to find out the truth. When he had rehearsed himself sufficiently, he called Nystrom. He wanted a real conversation, relaxed as far as possible, neither in his own office nor in Nystrom's, so he arranged to meet him on a bench in Oriole Park. He knew then, by Nystrom's failure to remark on such a place, that he had put Nystrom on guard after all, but he also knew that he was right. It made no sense, or rather, he refused to believe the kind of sense it made, but he knew he was right. Then he thought of something that both he and Nystrom might have missed, and he called City Hall and waited for them to find Constable Brennan. "Find a piece of typing that Lilliput sent out last year and have the lab compare it with the letters," he said.

"Last year?" The constable was appalled.

"That's right. Take your time. This may be your last job on this case."

NYSTROM WAS WAITING for him when he parked at Lascelles Boulevard, watching two teenagers play tennis. When Salter sat down next to him, two more tennis players appeared and sat on the bench behind, waiting for a court. Salter took a look around the park. There was a sprinkling of air hostesses and waiters lying about, getting an early tan, a number of old people, and some mothers with infants, but there was plenty of space to walk about without being overheard. Salter was reluctant to suggest a stroll in the direction of the baseball diamond because, since they had no dogs to walk, the scene would be too reminiscent of a couple of spies meeting in Hyde Park. The Belt line, a pedestrian walkway that had been created out of an old railroad, provided the answer, and they set off westward across the city.

"We've found out where those letters came from," was Salter's opening gambit.

Nystrom looked alarmed immediately. "And?" he asked.

"We have to do fingerprint tests yet, but I thought we'd have a little chat first, might save us some time."

Nystrom now looked ahead, waiting for Salter's next move. A lot depended on it. "Why did you do it?" Salter asked.

"Me!" Nystrom's lower lip began to vibrate, out of control. "Me! It wasn't me. It was ..." He held on to the name, biting savagely on his lip.

"Leese?"

"No!" Nystrom shook his head violently. "No, no!" Then the words began to pour out. "It couldn't possibly be David. I know that letter came from us but it couldn't have been David. It couldn't."

"Nor you?"

"No, no no."

"Or Mrs. Pearson?"

Now Nystrom could not speak, just shaking his head in misery.

Salter continued conversationally as if Nystrom was not out of control. "We have the letters, and we have some information that there was a contract out on Pearson."

"On *Pearson*? But ..."

If you rehearse every word, thought Salter, it's easy. Like making a speech. "I'll ask you again. Why did you do it?"

"I didn't, I told you. Not in a million years."

"What?"

"Kill Pearson, of course. Isn't that what you mean?"

"No. I mean tell that informer to call me."

They were crossing Avenue Road, and Nystrom looked as if he might collapse. Salter took his elbow and steered him past the traffic. When they were safely across, Nystrom asked, "How did you know?"

"Never mind that. I'm sure of it now. Why did you do it?"

Nystrom shook his head in refusal.

"Because you thought if the letters came from Lilliput, then Leese must have sent them?"

"Even if he *did* send them it was just like Vera. It doesn't mean he killed Pearson, but you people wouldn't..." His voice ended.

Now Salter fumbled slightly, not enough to affect the outcome, but enough to slow its arrival. "How did you find out the first batch came from Vera?"

"She told me. She tells me everything." The aside had given Nystrom some recovery time. "The point is..." he resumed, but Salter cut him off.

"It looks bad, though, doesn't it? He got the idea from Vera's letters and then saw how he could use it?"

Nystrom started to wail again, but Salter cut him off. "Take it easy," he said. "I wasn't going to tell you this but the letters didn't come from Lilliput."

Now Nystrom leaned against the door of one of the garages that lay beside the Belt line, immovable. "But you said they did?"

"No, I didn't. I said..."

Now Nystrom burst in. "Then it *wasn't* David. Oh, God."

"I didn't say it wasn't him. I said the letters didn't come from the bookstore. I'm going to get a sample from every typewriter you guys have access to. But I don't at the moment think you or Leese is involved, no, so there was no need for you to interfere, was there? What were you up to?''

"I was trying to make it look as if Pearson had intended to have Ruth killed and the killer chose the wrong day. I mean, it's possible, isn't it?''

Salter refrained from telling Nystrom how close their thoughts had been. "I guess so. So you really thought Leese did it?''

"Yes. *No*. After you came prowling around the garbage I realized what you were doing, and well, yes, I thought David might have sent the letters.''

"Why? There's only one possible reason.''

"I don't know, but I know he didn't have Pearson killed.''

"No, you don't. You hope he didn't.''

"He didn't.''

"So you had your actor friend call in. Pity he screwed it up. That wasn't what put me on to it. It was the timing. The first call came after I'd been in the bookstore, and I figured you probably saw me looking at that wastebasket. The second call came right after I'd talked to Mrs. Pearson. When you realized your actor friend had screwed up the message.''

"Yes, it was obvious that you were asking me about David. You're not very good at that kind of thing.''

Salter let this go. "Do you know what really made me suspicious? Your friend's accent. He sounded like someone from Brooklyn, maybe. Not Toronto, anyway.''

"I'll tell him,'' Nystrom said. "But you don't think David did it, then?''

Salter considered his next reply carefully. He didn't want Nystrom buying champagne all around in the Bellair Café before the file was as complete as he could make it. "Let's just say that on the basis of what I've seen of him, I am no more suspicious than I was at the beginning.''

Now Salter put his last question, the whole purpose of leading Nystrom along this trail. It was the question he hadn't been able to script properly, hoping to improvise on the basis of what Nystrom had said, and at least Nystrom had now had time to realize the implications of a typewriter and would have stopped looking so relieved. "Who's got the old typewriter?" he asked.

Nystrom moved his head through several planes as he considered the question. "The *old* typewriter?" Then as if a sad paper mask was being ripped off, his face exploded in joy. "Pearson!" he shouted. "Pearson had the old typewriter. He walked off with it and the filing cabinet. You've got the evidence haven't you, the letters came from the old typewriter. It's Pearson. He sent them. It is, I knew it.''

Salter stepped back as Nystrom appeared to be about to embrace him. "I said nothing of the kind." Nystrom stopped jerking about and watched Salter intently, certain he had found him out.

"Now. Who knew about the first bunch of letters?"

"How do you mean?"

"Who knew about them? Everybody in Yorkville?"

"Of course. The story was on television."

"The press didn't have the text of the message. How many people saw the letters? Did you?"

"Oh, yes. The morning they arrived we were all running up and down Yorkville comparing them."

"Who?"

"Everybody!"

"Pearson? Be careful. I don't want any bullshit."

Nystrom paused a long time before he replied. "Yes," he said.

"You sure?"

"No. I think so. I think he was in the coffee shop. I think so. But I'm not sure."

"Possibly?"

"Probably. He always ate breakfast there."

Salter said, "Do me a favor, will you? Go home. Pack a bag. Put a message on that machine of yours and go to New York or somewhere for a couple of days."

"I'll do anything you say. But why?"

"I am in the process of finally clearing Leese and Ruth Pearson, and you, I suppose. The way you've been acting lately, and the condition you're in now, I can't trust you. I could arrest you for the shenanigans of the last couple of days but that would be noisy and I want to be quiet. I want you out of the way."

"You can trust me, Inspector!"

"I can't trust you not to go singing and dancing around Yorkville, telling the world. I'd like to be sure that nothing, not a hint, gets out until I'm through. You'll have to trust that I'm clearing Leese, okay?"

"Oh, I will. Right. I'll go now. God, I feel wonderful. Thank you." He stared for a moment at Salter and once more Salter prepared to dodge. Then Nystrom turned and started to run along the path to his own car. Salter just had time to catch him and redouble his request that Nystrom stay silent before he roared away.

BACK AT THE OFFICE, Brennan was waiting for him. He had found a letter in last year's files from Ruth Pearson requesting permission to create a parking space in her front yard, and the type matched the type in the second batch of letters. "Go over to this place on Bloor Street," Salter told the constable, giving him Pearson's address. "You'll find a typewriter sitting on top of a filing cabinet in the living room. Take a full sample of the keyboard, take it over to the lab, and tell me tomorrow morning it's the same. Okay? Now we can both go home.''

The next morning he called in Madeline Crouch. When she arrived he took her over what she knew of the last twenty-four hours of Pearson's life. She had not seen him on the Friday evening because he had been busy, he said.

Picking up the bomb, Salter thought. "Did you speak to him?" he asked.

"He called me late, about eleven, to tell me where he could meet me on Sunday morning.''

"To help him move?''

"Move? No, we were going to Niagara-on-the-Lake for the day.''

"Did you know he was planning to move some stuff to the new store that weekend?''

"No, I told you we were going to Niagara. I wanted to go for a drive in my new little Honda. I don't know anything about moving.''

Salter thanked her for coming in. When she had gone, he called the owner of the building on Bayview Avenue which housed Pearson's store. From him he found out that Pearson did not even have the keys to the store. They were to have been handed over on Tuesday in exchange for a check.

"Didn't it bother you when he didn't turn up?'' Negligent as he was, Salter grabbed on to this bit of bad luck. He could now argue that if the owner of the store had inquired, these kinds of questions might have been asked a lot sooner.

"I didn't know about it. I was up at my cottage. I left my son in charge, and he just told me about it yesterday. I would have gotten around to it in a couple of days.''

Salter thanked him and hung up. It didn't take much thought now to construct the hypothesis that Pearson planned to rig the bomb, then call his wife to say that he did not need the van after all. Even that wasn't necessary, because after two or three days Pearson's wife would check the garage to see if the van had been returned, and finding it, activate the bomb. Pearson must have seen the combination of the street traders' threat and the royal visit as a golden opportunity to create an impenetrable mystery.

It was nearly overwhelming, but all still circumstantial. Was it enough for Wycke?

The bomb was the key to the possibility of proving it. He needed to show that Pearson could have detonated it accidentally while he was installing it, that he was inside the van when it was hooked up and somehow he touched the button. He went back to the explosives expert to get him to explain one more time how the bomb worked.

"It was electrically detonated. We found pieces of a battery, so it operated independently of the ignition, which means he didn't need any tools to hook it up, and that's good because we didn't find any at the scene. The thing was self-contained: The circuit went from the battery through the switch to the charge. So all he had to do was put the thing somewhere out of sight, connect the leads to the button, and then put the button where the next driver would have to depress it when he used the van. Under a wheel, somewhere like that."

"Or inside."

"I guess. Under the seat, maybe."

Salter left the office and drove to a Toyota dealer and asked the salesman to demonstrate a van. After the usual chat, he took the van for a ride, parking it around the block, and rehearsed the moves that Pearson went through. The front seat was suspended above the floor in an iron frame and could not be used to sandwich the button. The only other place was under one of the floor pedals, the brake or the gas. Pearson must have touched the pedal after the bomb was in place, perhaps slipped and fallen on it.

Salter thanked the salesman for his trouble and drove back to his office. Once more he sought expert confirmation.

"It's possible," the explosives expert said. "But not very likely, because he would have to have been very clumsy and very unlucky. The button isn't a hair-trigger—that would have been too dangerous. You would have to jam it pretty hard. He should have been able to put it all in place without jumping on it."

"But it is possible?" Much depended on it.

"Sure. It's possible."

"Maybe it was too lightly set. Did you press it?"

Solemnly the expert put his finger on the button and pressed, with no effect. "See? I can't even get it down. The explosion could have warped it, though."

"It looks all right to me. How much pressure does it take to get it down?"

The man looked at Salter with a patronizing air and put the button in a vise. He turned the handle slowly. After several turns the hollow button split, without descending a fraction. "Christ," the expert said. "The sucker won't move."

Then Salter had a vision. It was nothing much as visions go, but it was enough. He saw Pearson fumbling with the bomb on that Saturday afternoon in the garage, and his mind reached for the memory of the obsessed painter of Stoney Lake and his blow-ups of hidden details, and in the middle of his picture of Pearson holding the bomb was a tiny, clear picture of the button, creating a focus. He said, "Can you tear that off? Open it up?"

"Sure." He put the whole device into a clamp, and then, with a pair of needle-nosed pliers, peeled the button away from its base. He stared at what he saw underneath, finally looked up at Salter. "These terminals are soldered together. These wires are supposed to be separate and they make contact when you press the button, but these mothers are soldered together."

"Wouldn't that fuse it?"

"Fuse it? In this case it would make a hell of a big bang. If the circuit is complete already at the switch, anyone hooking it up would go *ka-boom* once the last connection was made."

"So it was rigged to kill him as he installed it?"

"It looks like it to me. It's a beautiful job."

Salter went back to Sergeant Crosbie to tell him what he had found.

"Let's squeeze Newton again," Crosbie suggested. "He hasn't come up with anything yet. Let's try him again. We won't get any hard evidence, but it might do for you."

NEWTON REFUSED TO TALK to them on their own grounds, offering instead to tell Salter and Crosbie his "thoughts" over a beer in the Pilot Tavern.

He was fat and jowly, with graying black hair lapping his collar, dressed in a stained safari suit. "Are we going to be taking this down?" he asked.

"Nobody's wired, Sticky," Crosbie said.

Newton looked at Salter. "This is just a chat," he said. "Some reflections, like. I haven't heard a thing. You understand?" He turned to Crosbie. "Does he understand?"

Crosbie nodded. Salter said nothing, glad he didn't have to deal with people like Newton often. Crosbie said, "Just tell us your thoughts."

In the end what Newton had to offer was a rambling scenario, full of repetitions that Newton was just guessing. "This guy Pearson was a bit of a blowhard, they tell me," he began. "I don't know the guy myself. They say, though, he was setting himself up a little bit, dealing a little. But the big thing is that he was probably telling a lot of people he was connected, bragging about it. He was hanging around a little, too, like some kind of groupie."

"Hanging around where?"

"Everywhere, I would guess. With the bikers, maybe."

They waited while Newton constructed the language of the next piece. "I figure that he might have started asking where he could get a bomb, a bit too loudly, like. Like a guy knocking on all the doors asking where the whorehouse is. If he found a bomb, he might have found someone to show him how to rig it."

They waited, but there wasn't any more from Newton. "Did you send him to the source?" Crosbie asked.

Newton looked impatient. "If I'd known you would ask a question like that, I wouldn't have bothered," he said. "I'm just trying to be helpful."

Crosbie stood up and Salter followed his lead. "Am I going to be hearing from you guys?" Newton asked.

"About Pearson?"

"Pearson's nothing to do with me," Newton said, with a directness he had not used so far. "I'm talking about this other stuff you claim you've got against me."

"Not this time," Crosbie said. "You'll hear in the end, though."

Newton said nothing and they left him there.

"IT'S A GOOD MESSAGE," Crosbie said. "As much as you'll get. Does it fit with the guy you've been investigating? Did he see himself as an operator?"

"Yeah, it fits all right."

"So the message is that Pearson was seen as a nuisance and someone got sick of him. So when he went to the wrong people for a bomb, he made them feel a little naked."

"So they showed him how to kill himself?"

"That's it. Newton didn't know what you'd found in the button. He just confirmed where it came from."

"So now we've got a homicide. All we have to do now is find out who rigged the bomb."

"That's right. Someone will tell us in five years' time. We'll find out eventually."

TWO DAYS LATER, a biker arrested on an impaired driving charge, faced with the appalling possibility of twelve months on foot, wanted to "put a patch" on the charge by trading information on how the bomb was rigged, but since he wasn't willing to say who rigged it, he was surprised to find out he had nothing to trade.

SEVENTEEN

"So Pearson cooked up the second letter to keep the pot boiling while he arranged his bomb," Orliff said. "He wanted the bookstore threatened. Right?"

"He sent the letters."

"All this for the insurance?"

"He was going down the tube. He could've been in hock to Newton for some drugs. He wasn't earning anything legitimately."

"And this Nystrom. He caught you sniffing around backstage?"

"He realized what I was after. And he knew how much Leese hated Pearson and he was afraid that Leese might just have set up the bomb. So he tried to con me with his informer pal. He was just being silly, but he helped me think out my next move."

"You going to charge him?"

"Not unless you say so."

Orliff shook his head. "Let's keep it tidy. His story isn't important. Might confuse the coroner. What we've got is solid enough. It was both."

"Both?"

"You were trying to prove that either Pearson was trying to kill his wife and had an accident, or that someone was trying to kill Pearson and succeeded. This is both. Nice. We can hand it over now, let them have the last bit. They're the experts on organized crime. Her Royal Highness has gone, everyone is back at work, and we have the evidence that Pearson was..." Here Orliff paused and a big smile appeared. "Hoist with his own petard," he ended. "You know what that means?" And then, in case Salter didn't, he continued. "It's a figure of speech. A metaphor, I think. Did you have to learn them at school? It means 'blown up with his own engine.' No, it's not a metaphor, it's the original, isn't it? I may be the only man who's ever used that literally." He sat back in his chair grinning.

"Would he have gotten away with it? If he'd killed her, I mean?"

"Probably. What do you think his plan was? Probably to call his wife on Saturday to say he didn't need the van after all. When the bomb went off he'd have said how lucky he was that he had changed his mind the day one of the street traders bombed the van. Or that his wife, or Leese or Nystrom, had left the bomb for him and gotten killed trying to dismantle it. We'd have been suspicious, but we'd never have a case. A lawyer like Tannenbaum would have laughed at us. It isn't that hard to kill someone and get away with it, so long as you keep your mouth shut." Orliff lined up the pages in front of him. "By the way, I can tell you what's happening after I'm gone. I don't know what your plans are now, but they aren't going to replace me."

"They rolling up the center?"

"No, they just aren't putting in a new superintendent."

"What happens to me?"

"Don't rush it. They are keeping the center and they're keeping you. You're in charge."

Salter ran the words through his head. "Who's my boss?"

"You'll be working directly for the deputy. As I have."

"I stay as I am?"

"You're being upgraded to staff inspector."

I'm in charge, thought Salter, and Orliff fixed it. Jesus Christ.

Orliff continued. "Look at it this way: The deputy wants to keep the center and he wants you, or anyway he doesn't *not* want you. But he's not replacing me. I think it's a budget thing. He's cutting his expenses by shrinking the cost of the center. Remember, the allowance he got for setting up the center he's probably made part of his general budget, so he can use the money somewhere else now but he wants to hang on to the center to justify his budget, and maybe just because he wants to."

All this, Salter realized, was a message in code, like Newton's. Orliff had been planning this all along, but even this close to retirement what he knew was confidential, and not to be shared with Salter.

"How long will you be around?" Salter asked.

"August thirtieth, I leave. It won't take me long to tidy up."

"Okay." Salter stood up.

"Okay, what? The deputy asked me to find out if you would be happy to stay."

"What did you tell him?"

"I told him I'd find out." Now Orliff stepped slightly over the line. "I told him I thought you would."

"Tell him I looked pleased, will you? Now I'm going on my vacation. Does he know?"

"When?"

"Next week. We're driving down to the Island. We have to put one of the kids on a plane first, then we're driving to Montreal for dinner, then down through the townships to Vermont and on to Bangor. We're going to spend about four days on the trip, just the two of us."

"A little honeymoon? Not too old for that?"

"We book into motels with vibrator beds. They help. We just want a few days on our own. See you in a month."

AT HOME, ANNIE LAUGHED. "I knew Orliff was up to something. I thought you would get the job."

"Why didn't you say?"

"I don't know. I guess I thought if I was wrong, you'd be disappointed." She considered her thoughts again. "But I think the real reason was that I thought it might make you careful."

ON THE EVENING before they left for the Island they listened to the first tape. They had intended to leave Seth alone with his project, but Salter's father had found an excuse to call them every day, and somewhere at the end of the conversation ask them whether they had heard a tape yet. So, after dinner, before Salter called his father to tell him they were leaving the next day, while Annie was assembling a mountain of luggage in the living room, Salter put the tape on a portable player and prepared to help Annie with the rest of the packing.

"My name is John Salter," the voice began, sounding like every pioneer they had ever heard. "I am—do I have to say how old I am? No? Right. I am retired and living in Toronto. I was born on Parliament Street during the Great War. That's the first one, son. My father and mother were Canadians, too. They were born here, but my grandfather came over from the old country, a place up in the north somewhere called Derbyshire, and he went out west like a lot of people did then. I had a picture of him once, but it's gone now. He's standing outside a store in Calgary—he worked in a hardware store—and he's got a six-gun on like the old cowboys used to have. It's just a joke, though, because the Mounties wouldn't have let him wear one. The fella standing next to him in the picture was allowed to wear a gun because he was a bank clerk and it's his gun he lent to my grandfather to have his picture taken with it.

"My father—your great-grandfather—was born in Calgary but he came to Toronto to look for work and that's how I was born here. I grew up here, right near here. We lived in the Beaches most of the time I was growing up. It's all changed now. Lots of Greeks live there now. Blacks, too, but at the time I'm speaking of it was all ordinary people like us. When I was sixteen I was an apprentice in the T.T.C. maintenance shop and there I stayed until I retired."

There was a long pause. Then Seth's voice came on. "When did you marry my grandmother?"

"Nineteen thirty-three. After she passed away I lived by myself until three years ago when I met this lady and we've been together ever since."

There was another long pause. "Seth is going to have his work cut out," Salter said.

Seth's voice came back. "What sort of food did you eat in those days?" "What do you mean?" the old man said. "Nothing but the best. Always a roast on Sundays. Why, what does your father tell you?" "Dad says he never tasted lasagna or clam chowder until he was married." "That's right. We wouldn't have had them in the house, not while I was working, and I never lost a day except for sickness in my life." "Did you always have enough to eat?" "Certainly, we did. So did your father. Not everybody did. I remember one family, the Bumsteads, like the fella in the comics, fourteen kids they had. Different religion from us, they were. One Saturday night I came by and they were all sitting round the table eating mashed potatoes. That's all they had. I was about eleven at the time."

And so it went on. As long as the old man was talking about the neighborhood and about other people, Seth got what he wanted. When Seth asked questions that related to the Salters' private life there was a defensive scramble, the verbal equivalent of the lace curtains of Salter's youth, put up to keep curiosity at bay. Salter sipped his beer, getting an insight into the value of oral history and the problems that lie with original sources. "Some of it's bullshit," he said to Annie. "He's wiping out all the stuff he thinks we should be ashamed of, like when he was laid off for six months and my mother went out cleaning houses to get the grocery money. We never went hungry, but we ate a hell of a lot of baloney. Why won't he tell the kid about that? That's the interesting stuff."

"Because he's defending his son's tribe."

"Against who?"

"His daughter-in-law's. He doesn't want Seth to get the idea that my family is superior to yours."

"Should I try to talk to him about it?"

"Don't say a word. Tell him the tapes are fascinating. If he talks long enough he'll forget he's being recorded and Seth will get the truth. Tape machines are insidious that way."

Before they went to bed he called his father to tell him how much he had enjoyed the tape.

"I didn't say too much, did I?" his father asked.

"No, Dad. Take your time. I've never heard some of that stuff before, about your father out west, for instance."

"It's funny. I've never thought about that for a long time. But once you start remembering, it all comes back. After Seth left I was remembering the stories your mother used to tell. She was an orphanage girl, you know, sent out here from England. Some of those kids were treated like slaves, but she was one of the lucky ones. She spoke well of the orphanage and of the people who took her in. She always said she worked a lot harder after she married me." He laughed.

"Dad, don't tell me. Tell Seth. On the tape machine."

"Should I? Would he be interested?"

"That's just what he wants."

"And you don't mind?"

"I want to hear it, too. It's my family."

"Right, then I will. Tell Seth we'll carry on when you get back. Nice lad that. Credit to you. Have a good holiday. Give her my regards."

"Liza Bennett is strong on story telling."
—*Inside Books*

SEVENTH AVENUE MURDER

Liza Bennett

When the head of a leading women's clothing manufacturer hangs herself with material from the new hosiery line, people will talk. Especially advertising people. Especially when the dead woman was about to cancel a huge deal from which many of them would have profited. Creative director for Merriweather Sportswear's new campaign, Peg Goodenough gets involved and is certain of one thing: Berry Merriweather did not commit suicide. Almost everyone at both the ad agency and at Merriweather seems to have had a reason for wanting the owner dead.

Available in February at your favorite retail outlet, or reserve your copy for January shipping by sending your name, address, zip or postal code along with a check or money order for $4.25 (includes 75¢ for postage and handling) payable to Worldwide Library:

In the U.S.	In Canada
Worldwide Library Mysteries	Worldwide Library Mysteries
901 Fuhrmann Blvd.	P.O. Box 609
Box 1325	Fort Erie, Ontario
Buffalo, NY 14269-1325	L2A 5X3

Please specify book title with your order.

 **WORLDWIDE LIBRARY**

SAM-1

ATTRACTIVE, SPACE SAVING BOOK RACK

Display your most prized novels on this handsome and sturdy book rack. The hand-rubbed walnut finish will blend into your library decor with quiet elegance, providing a practical organizer for your favorite hard- or soft-covered books.

"Adele Buffington can stand tall in the crowd of female sleuths."
—*New York Times*

AND BABY WILL FALL

MICHAEL Z. LEWIN

Indianapolis social worker Adele Buffington has her hands full with child welfare, a difficult daughter and a private-eye boyfriend. But when a man breaks into the office, copies a file and then disappears, followed by the discovery of a corpse with an unflattering note to social workers pinned to his lapel, Adele digs for answers. Was it a coincidence the murder victim had a name identical to one of her former employees? How did a missing mother and two daughters fit into the picture? The questions keep coming—and the answers lead to a web of death and danger that becomes more twisted by the minute.